THE VIRUS PROJECT

JOSEPHA W. QUINT

- THRILLER -

JOSEPHA W. QUINT

Corrections and editing by Angel Editing: www.angelediting.com

*" ... and you will know the truth,
and the truth will set you free."*

[John 8:32]

FACTS & FIGURES

54

Percentage of influenza patients aged between 10 and 17 who took antivirals and who are more likely to exhibit serious abnormal behaviour than those who did not take antiviral drugs. (Professor Yoshio Hirota, Osaka City University – 2006)

73

Percentage of patients hospitalised with Swine Flu in the United States of America, who had one or more underlying conditions, including asthma, diabetes, heart, lung, or neurologic disease, or pregnancy. ("Hospitalized Patients with 2009 H1N1 Influenza in the United States, April-June 2009", New England Journal of Medicine – 2009)

214

Number of countries and overseas territories or communities that have reported laboratory confirmed cases of the pandemic influenza H1N1 2009. (World Health Organization, as of 12/07/2010)

18,449

Confirmed number of deaths worldwide due to the Swine Flu virus. (World Health Organization, as of 01/08/2010)

215,000+

Population estimate of the city of Tenōchtitlān (known today as Mexico City), although some popular sources put the number as high as 350,000. It is believed that the city was one of the largest in the world in 1519. Only Paris, Venice, and Constantinople were larger.

48,000,000

Amount in Euros the French government will pay three swine flu vaccine makers for 358 million worth of H1N1 doses it cancelled. (Reuters – 23/03/2010)

50,000,000+

Number of people killed worldwide by the outbreak of Spanish flu, in 1918. (The Guardian – 18/01/2007)

65,000,000

Number of doses of pandemic vaccine that have been administered in over 16 countries, out of around 80 million doses that had been distributed worldwide. (World Health Organization – 19/11/2009).

CHAPTER 1. DEADLY VIRUS

Virus [noun] – a microorganism smaller than bacteria which functions as an infectious agent to cause disease in humans, animals, or plants.

(Excerpt from the Storyteller Dictionary)

1. Breaking News.

24th April 2009.

KNLTV News Calgary, CANADA.

The Mexican authorities have sent to Winnipeg's microbiology lab some blood samples from victims of a severe "influenza-like" illness that has already killed 60 people in Mexico. The lab is now trying to determine exactly what the virus is and why it is causing so many deaths. "The Mexican authorities had noticed unusual flu activity in March and April (a period when the flu season should be ending in the country)," a spokeswoman for the World Health Organization said, in a news briefing on Friday. "To date, there have been some 800 suspected cases with flu-like illness, with 57 deaths in the Mexico City area," she added.

The US Centers for Disease Control and Prevention said today that seven people in California and Texas have been diagnosed with a new type of Swine Flu. With both American states sharing a border with Mexico, sources at the WHO said that the United Nation agency is now concerned whether it may or may not be related to the illness in Mexico. The virus, the WHO says, is a never-seen-before mix of viruses usually found among pigs, birds, and humans. However, the cases are quite unusual since none of the patients were in contact with pigs before falling ill. This would suggest that it is an animal virus that is being transmitted from person to person.

*"The life of every person is like a diary
in which he means to write one story,
and writes another."*
– Sir James Matthew Barrie (1860 – 1937)

CHAPTER 2. JEAN-BAPTIST'S DIARY

Diary [noun] – a book in which one keeps a written
record of daily events, observations or experiences.

(Excerpt from the Storyteller Dictionary)

2. A new story.

Day 1 – 25th April 2009, 1.44 p.m.

Until this morning, I was working on a special report for my newspaper here in Mexico City about a high-level drug cartel member called J. Gamez, key member of the Beltran Leyva cartel, and in charge of negotiating deals with Colombian traffickers.

However, everything changed when I got the news that a deadly flu virus had killed up to 68 people across Mexico. So I decided to cancel my work... What was happening here seemed to be quite serious. A friend in the US even told me it could become a world pandemic since it had apparently already spread to a school in New York... Were these only rumours? What was going on?

Sitting on my big double bed at *Hotel Catedral* in the centre of Mexico City, I was searching on the Internet for some information about the virus, when another journalist sent me an email. A British Airways cabin crew member was taken to hospital with *"flu-like symptoms"* after falling ill on a flight from Mexico City to Heathrow.

This was going to be a big blow to the tourism industry if it was confirmed. According to different news websites and online blogs, even though the flu wasn't near tourist areas such as Cancun or Playa del Carmen, the news came across as if all of Mexico was affected.

I stood up for a moment. I needed to think. I tried to remember what I had witnessed on previous days. I tried to focus and the images became clear again. I remembered that I had noticed how the streets were almost empty compared to a normal Friday afternoon in the capital.

I grabbed my cup of coffee, trembling. My brain was suddenly running like a computer. Details of the few people in the streets, their appearance, and their strange looks... I should have known something was going on...

I switched on the television to see what they were broadcasting and although I couldn't understand a word of what was being said, I could see the fear in the Mexicans' eyes.

Suddenly, someone knocked at the door of my room. It was Bertrand, another French journalist I knew from when we covered the war in Iraq for the AFP together. He was carrying his laptop under one arm and his jacket on the other.

'Jean-Baptiste, did you hear about that strange virus that killed 68 people in Mexico?' he asked.

'Yes, what do you think about it? Is it an exaggeration?' I asked.

'Well, I spoke to some guys downstairs and they said there are rumours that Mexico City could be quarantined!'

As we were speaking, we could hear people running in the corridors.

'I also spoke to some Mexican staff at the hotel. They all blame the government for what's happening here, and they claim it's hiding something much more serious. They also think that the number of dead is far higher than we're being told. I've got a very bad feeling about all this…' Bertrand told me.

'Me too! Are you going to stay?' What I really meant was, *'Let's cover this story together.'*

'I'm afraid I can't. The agency recalled me just last night. They want me to go back to France to investigate the case of former Prime Minister De Villepin, who allegedly tried to manipulate a judicial investigation to prevent Nicolas Sarkozy from becoming president in 2007.'

'That sounds really interesting!'

3. Silence.

3.22 p.m.

I left the hotel and decided to walk to the Headquarters of *El Universal*, which is the most read paper in Mexico. I was going to meet Elena and Vicente, two fellow journalists who I met five years before in Barcelona. I wanted to discuss the controversy around the virus with them.

In the quiet streets of the capital, I saw some soldiers patrolling around. There were only a few people in the streets and all were wearing masks to cover their mouths. I had no idea whether these masks were actually effective though. Empty streets. Silence everywhere. Even the massive events and football games in Mexico City had been cancelled.

Once at *El Universal*, it was a bit surreal. I was walking around the offices and saw everyone wearing masks and they were thoroughly cleaning the PC equipment and surfaces. One could really feel a sense of uncertainty.

Through the window of their office, I saw my two Mexican friends talking to someone. I knocked on the door. Vicente, a very tall and slim young man, showed me in and offered me a seat. He quickly explained to me that they were interviewing a doctor about the Swine Flu virus. Dr Fernando Gutierrez was a small, bald, middle-aged man, with funny red and green glasses. He was wearing a classy black Eastern-inspired suit with a long jacket and mandarin collar, and a pair of Fratelli Rossetti Black cordovan ankle boots. He worked as a general practitioner at the Centro Medico Dalinde, a big hospital in Mexico City.

In incomprehensible Spanish, fortunately translated to me by Vicente, Dr Gutierrez was telling Elena that the situation was far from being under control. According to him, the media didn't actually reflect the situation and weren't reporting the truth about the virus.

'Dr Gutierrez says that even though vaccines are being distributed among medical staff, two of his colleagues died of the virus in less than six days. Tests are showing that the human swine influenza can be treated with anti-virals *Osneltavir* and *Zanimir,* which are sold under the names *Sanniflu* and *Velenza.* He also says that if the Swine Flu becomes pandemic, there won't be enough beds, ventilators, trained medical staff, and most likely drugs in most countries... If that's the case, food will be rationed out just like in wartime and a black market will appear. The distribution of most goods will be discontinued.'

Finally, Dr Gutierrez added that more than one thousand suspected cases had been reported nationwide and, strangely enough, most of the dead were aged 25 to 45. According to him, containing an outbreak of a disease in one limited area was possible, but once it was reported in widespread locations, the spread was then totally impossible to control.

Once their interview was over, the doctor left the newspaper office. My two friends insisted that something really strange was going on in Mexico with this outbreak.

'We're not able to properly investigate the cases of Swine Flu,' Elena explained, sitting in front of me in her stylish dark blue Prada suit. 'The authorities have forbidden us to interview the victims' families! As Mexican journalists, we can't try anything without triggering an alarm. Maybe as a foreigner, you could investigate further…'

Vicente crossed the four-metre-square room and sat by the window. The sun was shining outside, but nobody in the city was really enjoying it.

'Some Mexicans I spoke to today think the virus was deliberately cultured in a laboratory and released by some vaccine companies in order to sell their vaccine afterwards…' Vicente announced.

'Let's not forget that the 2007 outbreak of the foot and mouth disease in the United Kingdom did in fact originate from a government laboratory… shared with a US pharmaceutical company!' Elena added with a smile.

4. Breaking News.

The Donnaconian Press, CANADA.

Hospital official and Quebec's Health ministry have today confirmed that the province has no confirmed cases of Swine Flu. They have refused to comment on GKTV News report that two patients were placed in quarantine at Lakeshore General Hospital, in Pointe-Claire, near Montreal, as a precaution after they returned from Mexico. They were eventually released earlier today as both tested negative for the virus.

5. Breaking News.

Day 2 – 26th April 2009.

`The Daily Heliograph, UK.`

`Is the new virus spreading to the United States? Yes. Eight children in New York, two people in Kansas, and eight in California have already been infected by the Swine Flu, according to hospital reports. The World Health Organization (WHO) warns that the highly lethal mutant strain that is moving rapidly across Mexico could soon create a global pandemic.`

6. Bioterrorism?

1.28 a.m.

It was very late at night but I was still fully awake in my hotel room. I just couldn't sleep. I was trying to understand how such a virus could spread around the world so quickly. For the World Health Organization to use the word *pandemic*, it certainly meant that this virus was a very serious matter.

Just as I was plugging in my iPhone to charge after a long day out, I received a Google email alert on my black laptop. It said that on 17th April, the Mexican authorities had asked the Canadian-based National Microbiology Laboratory to find the cause of an outbreak of some severe respiratory illnesses. The NML was a division of the Public Health Agency of Canada, located in Winnipeg, and a member of the US Bioterrorism Response Network.

US Bioterrorism Response Network? Why bioterrorism?

Could a terrorist network such as Al-Qaeda be involved in the creation and spread of the Swine Flu virus? Why? Well, why not? I couldn't really imagine Bin Laden and Al-Zawahiri planning a terrorist operation where a global pandemic would put their own recruits at risk.

I suddenly remembered a video aired by Al Jazeera in February of an Al-Qaeda recruiter talking about smuggling anthrax into the United States via some tunnels under the Mexico border. He had also insisted that the network should ally itself with white militia groups and other anti-government groups interested in carrying out an attack inside the United States.

I decided to try to find the video online. Before I switched on the television to have some background noise, I decided to put on some music. Not loud enough to wake the neighbours up, though.

'MTV Latin America… why not? What's this? Ah, it's the playlist… half an hour of music only… that's perfect. Nothing to understand.'

I must confess that my Spanish was really very basic. So basic that Sarah, my English fiancée, never understood why I wanted to work in a country like Mexico, where I wouldn't be able to express myself and understand people properly. Well, I just always liked challenges.

The screen of my laptop was flashing after I typed two keywords on the *YouTube* search engine: *"Biological Attack"* and *"Al Jazeera"*. I sat on my bed and found the very same video I had seen back in February.

I watched it again. At the sound of the man's voice, a thrill of excitement ran through me.

'Four pounds of anthrax… in a suitcase this big… carried by a fighter through tunnels from Mexico into the U.S. is guaranteed to kill 330,000 Americans within a single hour if it is properly spread in population centres there. What a horrifying idea; 9/11 will be small change in comparison. Am I right? There is no need for airplanes, conspiracies, timings, and so on. One person, with the courage to carry four pounds of anthrax will go to the White House lawn, and will spread this "confetti" all over them, and then he will shout cries of joy. It will turn into a real celebration.'

After listening to these terrifying words, I thought that the terrorist lead couldn't be totally excluded. Or could it?

7. Whistleblower.

2.42 a.m.

I was spending some time on MIRC Internet chat rooms where people were talking about the Swine Flu virus. After three cups of coffee to keep me awake, I managed to speak with someone who claimed that she was working in the pharmaceutical industry.

She told me that I might be interested in a specific laboratory in Mexico City that worked on flu vaccines. She said that the laboratory belonged to the largest pharmaceutical company in the world that was entirely devoted to human vaccines, *Massoni-LaFleur*. It was a division of the French company *Massoni-Awattini Group*, the world's fifth-largest pharmaceutical company by prescription sales.

Why would I be interested in that laboratory?

'Maybe because Massoni-LaFleur distributes an influenza virus vaccine...' she answered on my computer screen. 'It's called *FluKilone* and it's recommended for vaccination against Type A flu viruses. Influenza A viruses are classified into subtypes on the basis of two surface antigens: hemagglutinin (H) and neuraminidase (N). Three subtypes of hemagglutinin (H1, H2 and H3) and two of neuraminidase (N1 and N2) are recognized among flu A viruses as causing the widespread human disease.'

I was a bit lost with this medical jargon, but it all seemed to make sense. She had just finished typing her last words when my interlocutor's nickname, *DoctorVanity1918*, suddenly disappeared from the screen. Could I trust someone I had just met online for a few minutes? Someone who claimed she was in the industry, but I had no proof of who she really was. Although she clearly knew a lot about the subject, anyone could actually find this kind of information easily anywhere on the Internet. Could she be a whistleblower? Could she be working for a competitor of Massoni-LaFleur, trying to get me into the wrong lead through false allegations? Or could she simply be a lunatic trying to make me believe her crazy stories?

Whoever she was, I decided to go on with my investigation and take on board some of her comments. There was certainly no harm in asking to visit the lab, or even just asking a few questions.

What could Massoni-LaFleur have to do with the Swine Flu outbreak in Mexico? I tried to understand… Could anyone vaccinated with their FluKilone against the Swine Flu contract a respiratory disease similar to the one in Mexico City, which would actually cause their death? The valuable US health-care website *RxMed* answered negatively. Could there be a link with the fact that Massoni-LaFleur's vaccine *FluKilone* was competing with the more famous *Sanniflu,* from its American market rival, *Borgia Labs Inc.*?

I really wanted to visit the lab in the morning if they would allow me to. I needed to speak to someone there to clarify my thoughts. In the meantime, I switched off the telly and my laptop, and went back to sleep. It was quite late already and I was going to have to wake up early to get to the lab as soon as they opened.

8. Breaking News.

KLY Sydney News, AUSTRALIA.

A group of students in New Zealand is currently being tested for Swine Flu after some of them suffered flu-like symptoms when returning from a trip in Mexico. When the three teachers and twenty-two senior students from Rangitoto College, the largest secondary school in New Zealand with over 3,000 students, returned to

Auckland after a three-week trip to Mexico, they
immediately started showing signs of influenza-like
symptoms, the Auckland Regional Public Health Service
(ARPHS) said today. They will remain in home isolation
as a precaution while tests are being carried out.

In Mexico, more than 80 people have died of Swine Flu
and over 1,300 have been infected by the virus. In the
United States, cases have now also been reported in New
York, California, and Kansas.

9. Pedro.

7.08 a.m.

I woke up, showered, had a quick continental breakfast in my
room, and got ready to go to Massoni-LaFleur's laboratory. It was located
in the city of Cuautitlán Izcalli, north-west of Mexico City. A last croissant
in the mouth, my iPhone in one hand, and the key of my rented Dodge
Caliber in the other, I was ready to go.

I had a last look at myself in the bathroom mirror only to see that I
looked very pale and drawn. What could I say about the big bags under my
eyes? Nothing I could do; I had slept for a bare four hours. My hair looked
as dull as my eyes, and my voice sounded a bit like Columbo's.

Down the lift. At the hotel reception, I met my good friend Pedro,
my Mexican interpreter; he had been helping me with translations since I
arrived in Mexico in March. Pedro was a small man with a moustache; he
was quite shy, very polite, always smiling and very well dressed.

'Where are we going today, Señor Duprés?' he asked as we got
into the car.

'We are going to visit a pharmaceutical laboratory in Cuautitlán Izcalli,' I answered, setting up the car navigation system to find the best route. 'Do you know that city?'

'I have been there a few times, yes. I know that nearly three quarters of the city's residents actually work in Mexico City. It often causes massive congestion on the Anillo Periférico, the only beltway. It might take us more than an hour and a half to get there, you know? Besides, it's Sunday and I'm not quite sure that the laboratory will be open.'

'Well, I think that with the Swine Flu virus spreading around, they will definitely be open. I need to ask them a few questions about the virus…'

'Are you not writing about the drug cartel anymore?' asked a fairly surprised Pedro, as I was starting the car.

I looked at him and explained the reason why I had decided to start investigating the events leading to the Swine Flu outbreak instead. Nobody knew what or who had initiated the deadly virus, and people were still dying of it every day. I thought that there was something really odd about it all, and one way of getting to the bottom of the story was to study the subject, examine the clues, inspect the places, analyse the proof, and consider any plausible theory.

Finally on our way to the lab, we quickly noticed that there were very few cars in the streets of the capital, even for a Sunday morning. For the last two or three days, public gatherings had been avoided. Public buildings, schools, cinemas, theatres, museums, and about eighty percent of the bars and restaurants were closed… Some people had abandoned their cars in the middle of the street, others their bikes. No one rode a bike in the street any more. No one took their dog out either. Mexico City, once one of the most polluted cities in the world, had probably now become the quietest city in the world.

Mexico City simply and terrifyingly looked like a ghost city.

10. Breaking News.

`Cairo31 TV News, EGYPT.`

`A twenty-six-year-old Israeli man has been admitted to hospital after having flu-like symptoms. He was returning from a trip to Mexico. Two French men, who had also just returned from Mexico, are now being kept under observation with the same symptoms. The World Health Organization advises all countries to be on alert for similar local outbreaks.`

11. At Massoni-LaFleur's lab.

9.11 a.m.

Cuautitlán Izcalli. When we arrived at the laboratory, we were denied access to the reception by a guard in a booth. He told Pedro that without an invitation, we wouldn't be entering the private property. According to the tone of his voice when he was speaking to Pedro, the very large chap with a small blue cap didn't seem to be the kind of person you wanted to mess with. Nevertheless, I asked Pedro to insist a little bit so that we could get someone to come and have a word with us outside the laboratory.

The guard phoned someone. After two minutes, a woman joined us at the gate. Her name was Dr Grizelda Torres. She was working for the Vaccine Department of Massoni-LaFleur and she spoke English. I was about to start my questions when Pedro and I realised that people in white coats were gathering at some of the windows of the laboratory to watch us.

'They all look very nervous, don't you think?' Pedro asked discreetly.

'They must know why we are here…'

My first question to Dr Torres was very simple. I looked deep in her eyes as I asked, 'Is there or is there not a vaccine against the Swine Flu virus?'

'There is currently no vaccine for the new strain of the Swine Flu virus, but the most severe cases can easily be treated with some antiviral medication,' she answered with a strong American accent. She went on to add, 'As it is unclear how effective any of the available flu vaccines will be to protect against the Swine Flu because it's genetically distinct from other strains, we need to work on a brand new vaccine. That's what we are doing here if you want to know! Even on a Sunday, as you can see!'

She looked quite nervous especially when I asked her about their laboratory and if there was any possible link between Massoni-LaFleur and the virus.

'Could it be possible for example that... let's say... someone working in your lab on some infectious diseases or on the Swine Flu virus itself... could have released this new virus by mistake?'

She immediately turned pale and started lecturing me.

'Our group is the world's fourth largest pharmaceutical company. Billions of doses of vaccines are provided by our company to immunise more than five hundred million people in the world. Do you know that our range of vaccines protects against twenty bacterial and viral diseases?

'I understand that. I have done my homework before meeting you and I know what your company does. Can you answer my question now?'

'We have nothing to hide and we are ready to offer our help to the Mexican authorities if needed...'

'I didn't mention the authorities, did I? Let me just reformulate my question: did the Swine Flu virus originate in Massoni-LaFleur's laboratory, here in Cuautitlán Izcalli? It's a simple question really.'

Dr Torres was very angry with me asking her that question, and she clearly wasn't going to answer. She turned to Pedro and switched to Spanish. She asked him to take me away from the laboratory because I would simply not be allowed inside. As she returned to the facilities of Massoni-LaFleur, I had even more doubts in my mind than before.

Was Dr Torres trying to hide the truth? Was Massoni-LaFleur the actual origin of the virus? Could it be that easy?

An hour and a half later, back in Mexico City, I thanked Pedro for his help and told him I was going to go for a little walk around my hotel to think… I would meet him later.

12. Theories.

11.47 a.m.

I was walking down the streets towards the Mexico City Metropolitan Cathedral, thinking back to when I first visited Mexico City with Pedro in March. He had taken the role of tour guide as he told me about the cathedral.

'It is the largest and oldest cathedral in the Americas, with its sixteen chapels. It is situated on top of the former Mexica sacred Templo Mayor, one of the main temples of the Mexica in the capital city of Tenochtitlan, which is now known as Mexico City. The Mexica settled in the Basin of Mexico in about 1200 and they spoke *Nahuatl*. Since the eighteenth century, the term *Aztec* has been popularly but incorrectly used to describe the Mexica civilization.

'The cathedral was built soon after the Spanish conquest of the old city, Tenochtitlan, and Hernán Cortés supposedly even laid the very first stone of the original church personally.'

As I was passing the cathedral, I thought about the different theories that had come to my mind since I met Dr Torres at the laboratory earlier. I sat on a bench on Plaza de la Constitución, in front of a monument built in memory of the founders of the former Mexica capital, and switched on my laptop. I then tried to put my thoughts into words.

First theory. Human cases of Swine Flu have occurred because of contact with pigs. Human-to-human transmission has also occurred, but it is rare and well monitored for the moment. It could be that another infection of some kind broke out in Mexico City, and that infection could have actually helped spread the virus… In this case, the causes of the Swine Flu outbreak could be absolutely natural.

The normally crowded square was exceptionally empty of people. No children were playing around. No tourists were feeding the pigeons. Only a few soldiers wearing masks were standing by the monument.

Second theory. A pharmaceutical laboratory in Mexico City (it could really be any lab at all…) could have mistakenly let the virus out of its facilities while making secret experiments. In this case, no one would want to be blamed for it. They would keep it secret, and the only way to deal with the virus would be containment (through quarantine, etc.). I know that such tests have already been executed; I remembered seeing a newspaper story about it a few years ago.

13. Archives.

BTVB News, UK. (September 2006)

A team of scientists in the United States have reconstructed the deadly 1918 flu virus in an experiment that has given a new and better understanding into how the virus became a world pandemic at the beginning of the nineteenth century. When infected with the recreated virus in the laboratory, a severe immune system reaction was triggered in mice. The team believes that the fierce

reaction, which remained active until the animals'
death a couple of days later, could have provoked the
body to begin killing its own cells, making the flu
even deadlier. It has also been noticed that at the
same time, the mice suffered a severe lung disease,
characteristic of the virus.

14. More theories.

Seven birds flying across the sky. Was that a sign?

Third theory. As prevention for the seasonal pig flu in Mexico (direct transmission from pigs to humans is rare, with only twelve cases in the United States since 2005), all hospital staff were vaccinated. However, one vaccine could have been contaminated with an active virus. Therefore, someone could have been inoculated with the deadly virus, and for whatever reason, it might have then mutated and become transmissible from human to human…

An old Mexican woman suddenly approached me and as she was shouting at me in Spanish, she gave me a small yellow and grey leaflet, before being led away by two soldiers who clearly thought she was disturbing me. The leaflet bore a title that even I could understand thanks to the apocalyptic illustration above it: *"¡El fin del mundo esta muy cerca!" ("The end of the world is coming!")* I needed to focus on my work.

Fourth theory. The spread of the Swine Flu virus was intended. It could be the latest invention in the war between pharmaceutical companies. One of them would purposely let a virus get out of its facilities so that the Swine Flu virus becomes pandemic. Countries all over the world would then rush to stockpile the brand new vaccine that only that company could produce. In a period of recession, it always helps to make money.

While browsing on the Internet, I found that a company called *Borgia Labs Inc.* had discovered the antiviral Sanniflu and was holding its patent. In 2005, after fearing a world Bird Flu pandemic, not less than sixty countries ordered Borgia Labs' vaccines. According to the magazine *Forbes*, Sanniflu sales were $258million in 2004 and exceeded $1 billion in 2005. This was despite the Food and Drug Administration, or *FDA* as they prefer to be known, amending the warning labels of Sanniflu to include possible side effects such as delirium, hallucinations, and other related behaviour. What a good business anyway! What would they do without viruses?

I also discovered that the former US Secretary of Defence was Borgia Labs' chairman from 1997 to 2001 and his holdings were estimated at $5-$25million. Then in November 2005, the President of the United States requested the Congress to fund $1.4 billion for government purchases of antiviral drugs. The Secretary of Defence must have been exulted, and so was his purse too!

Nobody actually knew what the full potential impact of the pandemic was, but experts had already warned that it could cost millions of lives worldwide. The Spanish flu pandemic in 1918, caused by the H1N1 strain, killed 50 million people…

The old woman was still screaming, causing me to look up from my laptop. The two young soldiers looked rather ill at ease with her behaviour, then without warning, a small military van appeared. Five soldiers jumped out of the vehicle, grabbed the poor woman, threw all her leaflets on the floor, and violently shoved her into the van. As she was still not cooperating, one of them kept her quiet by knocking her out with his submachine gun. The van disappeared and the other two soldiers immediately started burning the leaflets in a bin.

I felt totally useless watching the scene from a distance, sat on my wooden bench. I could understand that the authorities of this country wanted people to stay calm and not panic because of the spread of the virus. I could also understand that the authorities preferred the Army to be deployed around the country to avoid mass panic. Was it on behalf of the

Mexican authorities that such abuse had been used against a totally harmless old woman? The soldiers' behaviour simply disgusted me.

I decided to leave the Plaza right away and return to my hotel room. I needed a little nap before searching for some clues to prove that one of my theories could be right.

I also wanted to watch a football game live on telly in the afternoon: Lille versus Marseille, at 3 p.m. As I was born in Carcassonne, in the south of France, I could only support Marseille.

15. The phone call.

5.08 p.m.

I stood up from my bed after having watched a beautiful game. Marseille registered their sixth Ligue 1 win against Lille, who was going to ruefully look back at missed chances in the game that ended 2-1. Time for a little snack.

My mobile phone rang. It was my colleague, Bertrand, from the AFP.

'Jean-Baptiste, are you still investigating the Swine Flu thing?' he asked.

'Yes. Why?'

'Well, I'm at Heathrow Airport, just back from Mexico. I just wanted to let you know that after my plane landed, all passengers were held on board for about forty minutes while two health inspectors checked everyone for any signs of the virus.'

'Really?'

'Really!'

'But as far as I understand it, anyone could have brought the disease into the UK without having developed any symptoms yet since it can be carried for a week before its effects begin to show.'

'I know that a couple of people put their hands up when the inspectors asked if anyone had any symptoms, but they eventually let everyone go. They made us write our details on the back of our ticket stubs just in case they needed to contact us, but in the end, they didn't even take them.'

Why would the UK authorities send inspectors to check the health of passengers of a flight from Mexico and then let everyone go? They should have kept them all in quarantine to avoid a possible spread of the virus in the country. Unless they had another agenda in mind. Were they actually looking for something else, or perhaps even someone else?

Bertrand interrupted my musings as he continued, 'I remember overhearing the inspectors asking the passengers with symptoms a few questions about their whereabouts during their stay in Mexico, as well as some odd questions about their nationality and their family's origins…'

Then the telephone abruptly hung up, probably because he had used all his credits, I assumed.

What could the passengers' origins have to do with whether they would or would not be infected by the virus? I couldn't help but think that there was something increasingly intriguing about the Swine Flu outbreak, and I could now see the outlines of a secret scheme, some sort of worldwide conspiracy involving governments and laboratories. Could I be right?

"For each illness that doctors cure with medicine, they provoke ten in healthy people by inoculating them with the virus that is a thousand times more powerful than any microbe: the idea that one is ill."
– Marcel Proust (1871-1922)

CHAPTER 3. DEATH

Diary [noun] – a book in which one keeps a written
record of daily events, observations or experiences.

(Excerpt from the Storyteller Dictionary)

16. Breaking News.

Day 3 – 27th April 2009.

The Daily Profess, UK.

There are at least seven more countries investigating
suspected cases of Swine Flu, while others are checking
on tourists who may display the symptoms. About 1,300
people altogether are thought to have been infected by
the deadly virus. Professor Nigel Dimmock of Warwick
University said, "In the worst-case scenario it could
kill two percent of the world's population." According
to him, this flu has the potential to be bigger than
the Spanish influenza that killed 50 million people in
the world in 1918.

17. The stairs…

8.22 a.m.

I woke up this morning with the telly on. I couldn't speak a word of Spanish, but when I read the headlines on the screen saying, *"Suman 103 decesos"*, I understood that the death toll here had risen to 103. I also noticed that every commercial break was giving some information on the symptoms of the Swine Flu and some messages along the lines of, *"Go to the doctor."*

But it seemed that the actions of the Mexican government to contain the virus didn't match the official statistics. Were they just being overly cautious or were things a lot worse than what the public was being told?

Before going downtown and speaking to some people, I decided to check on my laptop for some more information about the virus. I realised that strangely enough as far as I could tell, the only cases of death from the Swine Flu were located and concentrated in Mexico City and its surroundings… Why was that? Why was the virus not affecting any other part of the country, only Mexico City, the State of Mexico, and San Luis Potosi?

I couldn't find the missing pieces of this puzzle. I took my breakfast without any hurry. I didn't have any more leads to build my investigation on, though I could really feel there was something to be discovered here in Mexico City. But what?

My cup of coffee in one hand, a slice of bread and butter in the other, I had a look out at the street from the window of my hotel room. It really seemed like a ghost town. At rush hour, the streets were totally deserted.

There were still many small buses running around, but they were totally empty of people. For the very first time since I arrived in March, I could hear the birds singing. That's how silent Mexico City was, and that was almost scary actually.

A few pedestrians appeared on the corner of the street wearing those blue surgical masks given away by the Army during the last few days. Everyone was still keeping their distance. Among these courageous people, I saw two friends on the same pavement greeting each other from a distance and talking to each other using their mobile phones. Then one of them crossed the road so that they wouldn't walk too close to each other.

I couldn't stand looking out the window any longer. I had to go out too. I quickly took a shower, changed my clothes, and made my way outside. As I was waiting for the lift, I saw people taking the stairs so that they wouldn't have to squeeze together in the confined space of a lift. I then decided to follow them wearing my own mask for the first time. It felt like being at the hospital ready for surgery… it was weird! Going down the endless stairs, I promised myself to never choose a room on the fifth floor anymore.

Most tourists in my hotel were journalists covering the Swine Flu story for some European and American TV channels, and some British and Latin-American newspapers. We all met on the stairs and the conversation quickly started.

'The Mayor, Marcelo Ebrard, is apparently considering shutting down the entire public transport system!' announced one of my Brazilian stairs mates.

'Well, in February, I was in London and the heavy snow managed to get the complete shutdown of the city's bus network… that was amazing!' a colleague working for CNN joked.

'You can't compare the two!' A Mexican cameraman halted them, and everybody stopped walking too. 'This is serious! People are dying because of a virus that spreads like the plague! You can't make jokes like this! Do you hear me? Respect these people a little bit!'

The Brazilian and another Mexican attempted to calm him down. A few words in Spanish and we could all go down the stairs again. The friction between the two men reflected the nervous mood people were in and the increasingly tense atmosphere in Mexico City.

18. The situation is really bad.

8.58 a.m.

As I left the hotel, I was about to get into my car when Pedro called me on my mobile phone.

'Señor Duprés, I just spoke to some friends working in a hospital here in Mexico; they told me that the situation is really bad. Even doctors and nurses are dying of the Swine Flu now. But all the staff have been told not to talk about it… It also seems that they all knew about the flu at least a week before the alert was issued.'

'Why is it that I'm not surprised?' I asked ironically.

'They told me that they aren't sure whether pharmacies have stocked enough antiviral drugs. Anyway, doctors aren't even expecting the drugs to have any effect on contaminated people, not even with high doses!'

'Well, does that mean that people are being given drugs just for the sake of giving them something?' I thought aloud. 'Or just to sell them something?'

Pedro finished by telling me his friends had told him the mortality rate in Mexico was higher than reported by the authorities. At least three to four patients were dying every day of the Swine Flu.

I asked Pedro to meet me later to tell me more about his friends as I jumped into my Dodge. I wanted to meet someone downtown who was hopefully going to give me some clues to prove whether one of my theories was right. In the meantime, I had a text message conversation on my mobile from a friend of mine, who was a radio journalist in Spain.

Miguel: Hi JB! I know you investigate Swine-Flu in Mex. Here in Spain 1st case now confirmed. It's 1st confirmed case in Europe!

J.B.: Thks Mig! Investig going nowhere yet. Too many leads. Not sure what to believe. Visit 1 lab… no help!

Miguel: My advice: trust no one. Only trust your instinct! It worked last time in Iraq!

J.B.: That was different. It was war. This time it's pandemic!

Miguel: A serious one it seems… Keep me posted. Take care.

J.B.: Tks again.

Miguel: Good luck JB!

19. Breaking News.

Shares Watcher, USA.

The deadly virus outbreak in Mexico has rocked the markets all around the world on Monday, as traders fear a repeat of SARS, the epidemic that devastated Asia six years ago. Airlines, cruise operators, and travel agencies are suffering the most. Since cases are now spreading across continents, the World Health Organization has decided today to raise the level of its alert to four, two levels below the WHO's pandemic level.

Magnus Press Agency, UK.

Early this Monday, the FTSE 100 share index was down
1.2% under growing concerns that the Swine Flu
outbreak, which has already killed 103 people in Mexico
alone, could well become pandemic.

The Custodian, UK.

Postpone nonessential travel to the United States or to
Mexico. That's the health advice given to Europeans by
the European Union's Health Commissioner this Monday,
after a meeting with the EU foreign ministers on the
subject of the Swine Flu virus. This comes as Spain
reported the first confirmed case of the virus in
Europe – it is also the first case outside North
America.

20. DoctorVanity1918

9.22 a.m.

I arrived near the Basílica de Guadalupe in the historic centre of
Mexico City and parked my car behind the building in a small narrow
street called 5 de Mayo. My car was just beside a sign on a wall reading
"Respete mi entrada y yo respeto su coche", even I could easily
understand it meant something like, *"Don't park in front of my door and
I'll respect your car"*. That was an interesting warning.

Earlier this morning, I had received an email from my anonymous
contact on the net, *DoctorVanity1918*. She wanted to meet me in the
Basilica at ten o'clock. I was more than on time. I was supposed to register
at the Information Centre to the guided visit of the old church and wait
until she showed up. So I registered and the tour started on time.

The guide was an old chap with grey hair, dressed in a suit that looked like it came straight out of the seventies. He spoke only Spanish. No need to say that I got lost after his first few words.

After ten minutes of the visit with about twenty other tourists, who were all Spanish speakers, I started to get a bit bored. I could understand neither the history nor the subtlety of the rich decoration of the site, nor even what the paintings inside the church reflected. I removed my mask as none of the other tourists were wearing theirs.

I sat on my own on a pew and started admiring the old ornaments, the paintings on the walls, the paintings on the ceilings, the statues, the golden chalice… I also noticed some people in masks probably praying to the Virgin of Guadalupe for deliverance from the deadly virus.

That's when a beautiful young woman came along. She was in her twenties, tall, and brunette with fairly long hair. She had a pert nose and her eyes were an emerald colour. As she smiled at me, a ray of light coming through the stained glass of the church made her look like an angel with an aura around her. That was something!

'Do you know the origin of the name *Guadalupe*?' she asked me in perfect English, as she sat next to me on the bench while the rest of our group gathered in front of a painting of the Virgin Mary.

'Not really,' I answered mechanically, a bit hypnotised by her charming ways. 'Do you?'

'It is quite controversial actually. There are different opinions or theories… For example, a report made in the sixteenth century says that when she appeared to Juan Diego on the hill of Tepeyac, on 9th December 1531, Mary identified herself as Guadalupe. But some historians say that Guadalupe is in fact a corruption of a Mexica name. *"Coatlaxopeuh"*, in Nahuatl, means *"Who Crushes the Serpent"*. The serpent is one of the Mexica gods, Quetzalcoatl, who Mary is said to have crushed by inciting the conversion of the indigenous people of Mexico to Catholicism. Finally, other historians believe that this shrine was originally dedicated to the

Spanish Lady of Guadalupe in Extremadura, Spain, not to the Mexican Virgin worshipped today.'

'Which is the right theory?' I asked, as she discreetly handed me a small book with a blue velvet cover with a small engraved cross in its centre.

'Nobody knows. No one was there at the time to see and report it, I think…'

I opened the book and surreptitiously read a handwritten email address on the very first page:

DoctorVanity1918@gmail.com

There was also a chemical formula:

$$H1N1 = HA + NA + PA + PB1 + PB2 + NP + M + NS = XAU$$

I closed the book. I had immediately recognised the *H1N1* bit as the formula name of the Swine Flu virus. The rest of the formula was far too complex for me, totally beyond my comprehension. I also recognised the *XAU* bit; it was the currency code for gold. But what did gold have to do with the Swine Flu?

At least it was confirmed that the angel sitting by my side was in fact my contact. She was *DoctorVanity1918*. She had tried to give me hints all along. I had so many questions to ask her, but my mind suddenly went blank. She continued anyway.

'You know, the Virgin of Guadalupe has been given the titles *"Queen of Mexico and Empress of the Americas"* and *"Patroness of the Americas"*. She is a really important symbol for the Catholics in this country.'

The young woman was constantly looking around, checking the time on her small silver watch. I asked her a question.

'Could it be that the building of this shrine was built on secrets?'

'This sanctuary has been built on secrets and lies. But secrets and lies always end up being exposed, don't they?'

She stopped when an old man's walking stick fell on the floor and the loud noise echoed round the church. Then she turned to me again.

'Money has always driven good and bad intentions, as well as great ambitions. It was already the case in 1531 when they built this church under Spanish rule, and it is still the case today... An example: in November 2006, the Basilica authorities announced they had plans to place a Domino's Pizza franchise within the site. That meant more than a hundred merchants who sell traditional and local food on the site would have to be removed. The authorities of the borough then rejected the request arguing that they had legal permits to work there. The franchise is still awaiting approval and if they ever get the green light, the Basilica is likely to get nearly a million pesos profit!'

'Money...'

Our group had now moved to another section of the old church. She asked me to follow her example and kneel on the mat in front of the next seating bench as if I was going to pray. A few people were actually praying four or five pews ahead of us.

As she kneeled first, I had time to have a quick look at her. She was wearing a long beige and black dress with fancy beige high heels and carrying a small black Louis Vuitton bag. She smelt of vanilla.

I kneeled by her side. Since the beginning, she had been using analogies to lead me to somewhere, but I needed to ask her straight questions to get straight answers. I spoke to her in a whisper.

'No one outside Mexico died of H1N1 until now. The world could be on the brink of a pandemic. Can the virus actually acquire the ability to spread easily among the population?'

She looked at me for two seconds, smiled, and whispered back.

'In 2005, U.S. scientists in Atlanta began experiments to provide answers to the same question about the Avian Flu. The work didn't indicate how soon a pandemic could start and there was no guarantee the virus would evolve the way they predicted. They mated H5N1, the Avian Flu virus, and human flu viruses in a specific process known as reassortment. The result was then tested in animals thought to be good substitutes for humans to see how it was reacting; they took note of the severity the disease provoked.

'In other words, the researchers deliberately engineered viruses of pandemic potential in laboratories. It was a dangerous experiment, but it was also fully justified by the World Health Organization, who had been pleading for months for qualified research facilities to undertake these tests. The Atlanta scientists worked in high containment laboratories with special features designed to protect both the workers and the world against a viral escape.'

She stopped as a priest crossed the hallway, then she continued her story.

'Still, lab accidents can happen. Since 2003, four lab workers in Asia have become infected with SARS and one spread it beyond the walls of his laboratory. In 2004, a Russian lab worker died after accidentally infecting herself with the Ebola virus… The Atlanta scientists mixed genes from H5N1 with genes from circulating strains of human flu to see which combinations produce viruses that grow and infect. The seasonal flu virus, H3N2, was the first priority, until H1N1, a mild descendant of the strain that caused the Spanish flu of 1918, reappeared in Thailand in 2004.'

'How does it work?'

'Well, reassortment can be performed in two ways. Scientists can use reverse genetics, a procedure that allows them to custom-make a virus with a predetermined constellation of genes from each parent virus. Or they can simultaneously infect tissue culture with two different viruses and see what results they get. Some gene combinations can be produced and others cannot.'

'Could the current Swine Flu virus have been produced in laboratories through reassortment?'

'Definitely.'

'Did it happen?'

'You are the journalist… it's your turn to investigate…'

That was it. She stood up without warning and walked away without saying anything else. Not even a goodbye. Nothing.

21. Archives.

KNLTV News, USA. (December 2004)

Pandemic experiments are to be conducted at the Centers for Disease Control (CDC), in Atlanta, in the new year. This is because experts fear that the world could be on the brink of an influenza pandemic; a consequence of the highly virulent Avian Flu strain ravaging poultry stocks in Southeast Asia. The question is: can the H5N1 strain actually develop the ability to propagate easily to and between humans?

The scientists will breed the H5N1 virus and some human flu viruses together in a process known as reassortment. That is to say that the CDC scientists will deliberately engineer viruses of pandemic potential by mixing H5N1 with genes from human flu to see what combinations could be dangerous for us. The researchers insist that even though it is high-risk work, it is definitely crucial to the understanding of viruses.

A mild modern descendant of the Spanish flu of 1918 has recently been very active in Thailand. The virus, known

as H1N1, will therefore be one of the viruses the CDC
will be able to work with.

22. The bald men.

10.46 a.m.

Since yesterday, after meeting with Dr Torres at Massoni-LaFleur's laboratory, I had noticed that two black cars had been following my every move. Two Mazda CX-9 cars with tinted windows, the SUV type of car.

I thought that I was possibly getting into something secret and perilous that somebody didn't want me to uncover... I sat in my car, put my belt on, started the car, looked in the rear-view mirror showing the two Mazdas behind me, and suddenly pressed the accelerator to the floor.

My car's GPS was on. I turned to Calzada De Los Misterios, a big road that adjoined the Basilica, and skidded my car with my tyres rasping on the road. Fortunately, there wasn't any other car there as I managed to keep control of the Dodge. Still pressing on the accelerator, I quickly got out of the neighbourhood, with no sight of the two black cars behind me. It wasn't really difficult to know whether a car was following you: there were hardly any cars in the city streets. I went past the stalls of Antojitos Mexicanos usually selling snacks to pilgrims and tourists going to the Basilica, but now they were closed because of the Swine Flu.

I was still driving really fast, afraid that the two cars would catch me, when I came to a set of traffic lights. Instead of slowing down on the two-lane, I decided to push the accelerator even more and jump the lights. There were no pedestrians, children, or bicycles around. No cars were crossing and no police car started chasing me either.

I was approaching a second crossroad when I realised the two cars had reappeared behind me at a distance. I was actually far from having lost them. They accelerated. I could now discern there were about four or five men in black suits and sunglasses in each car. No masks. Even though I knew I was certainly getting seriously involved with something potentially big in my investigation, I still couldn't imagine who those men were. Did they simply want to scare me? I had hardly found out anything at all about the Swine Flu…

One of the two Mazdas unexpectedly accelerated and quickly came up behind me, then beside me. The tinted window slowly rolled down and a bald man with sunglasses appeared, pointing what I recognised as an M4 Carbine directed towards me. He started shooting at my car, shattering all my windows. Then the driver tried to push me off the road three or four times without success. I wasn't a bad driver after all.

This wasn't just about scaring me anymore. They actually took shots at me and tried to crash my car… They wanted me dead.

As they were still by my side at the next crossroad, I decided to ignore the stop sign. A big white truck suddenly crossed my way and collided into the front right side of my Dodge. I lost control of my vehicle and it span round twice before being thrown violently against a wall. Fortunately, my airbag blew up immediately and prevented me from hitting the wheel.

I quickly recovered from the accident. I was still a bit shocked and dizzy, but as I looked at the state of the car, my first thought was of the rental company, who was going to charge me a lot of money for the repairs the poor car would definitely need.

The Dodge wouldn't move, the engine wouldn't start, and smoke was coming out of the bonnet since it had been perforated by a dozen bullets. I had to leave the car behind me and walk. As I opened the door, I noticed that the two Mazdas had missed my accident and driven off. It was my chance to escape from these guys. I couldn't go back to my hotel as I was sure they would have somebody waiting for me there. I had to contact Pedro and ask him for some help. In the meantime, I needed to hide. Not being too familiar with Mexico City, not being able to speak a word of

Spanish, and with only my iPhone and the blue book on me, it wasn't going to be easy.

23. The taxi.

11.22 a.m.

Having a GPS application on my iPhone was really a great help. It certainly saved my life. I ran across the Calzada De Guadalupe, realising my left foot was injured slightly; it was possibly only a sprain, nothing major. I could still run.

I resolved to take a taxi as I noticed the two Mazdas were after me again. A white vehicle stopped next to me. I jumped into the car and stammered my request to the driver.

'Hum... to the... hum... Basilica De Guadalupe... por favor!'

'*¿A cuál Basílica quiere ir exactamente?*' asked the young driver, turning to me with his fancy sunglasses and a mask with a big smile drawn on it.

As I closed my door, I looked at him for two seconds without a word. I didn't understand his question. I looked at the window behind me and saw that the two cars were about to catch me. That's when I urged him to start driving.

'They will get me! Go! Go! Go!'

Without asking any more questions, the driver immediately turned back to the wheel, driving away as quickly as he could in the deserted streets of Mexico City. Looking at me through his rear-view mirror, he seemed a bit worried.

'*¿Por qué están siguiendonos estos dos automóviles?...*'

Silence. I didn't understand a word he was saying.

'You is police?' he asked in bad English.

'No, I'm not the police… I'm a journalist… These two cars behind us are trying to catch me, that's why I need you to drive fast, otherwise they are going to kill me!'

'You is police?' he asked again, as if he didn't understand anything I had just said. His English was probably as bad as my Spanish.

'*Periodista?*' I tried, using my iPhone dictionary application.

As we were accelerating on the four-lane avenue, the Mazdas were getting closer and closer. Once again, their tinted windows slowly rolled down to let my bald friend and one of his sunglasses-wearing mates appear with an M4 Carbine each. When my driver saw the two assault rifles through the rear-view mirror, his driving suddenly became even more shaky and hazardous.

They started shooting again. I just had time to lean down on my seat when all the windows were shot to pieces. My driver got so scared that he lost control of our car for a few seconds. We were about to crash into a bus when he managed to get a good grip on the wheel and narrowly avoid the accident. As for the other two cars, they were still chasing us. One of them pushed us twice to crash against parked vehicles, but my driver was really good and as we reached the end of the street, he sent the other car flying into the window of a MacDonald's restaurant.

As we were going to turn right on another street, I ordered him to stop the car.

'Stop here! Stop!'

He shouted something in a furious voice; I imagine it was about the damage to his car so I left a couple of thousand-peso notes on my seat, before running away from his car.

'Really sorry for the damage, hope this money can help you somehow!' I called after him.

I climbed up the stairs and ran towards the new Basilica. It didn't take long for my driver to grab the money and make his way out of the neighbourhood as fast as he could.

At the same time, the last Mazda stopped behind me. Six tall bald men with sunglasses and black suits stepped out of the car. Four of them immediately came after me. Two stayed behind as if they were waiting for more cars to arrive.

24. Hiding.

11.40 a.m.

I managed to discreetly get inside the new Basilica. I decided to hide on its roof next to the cross, as they wouldn't immediately think about looking for me there. I desperately needed to call Pedro and ask him to come help me. As I was dialling his telephone number, I could see the four men in black patrolling the gigantic Plaza below me, in front of the two Basilicas, still looking for me.

Pedro, who lived in Tlalnepantla de Baz in the north-west of Mexico-City, told me it would take him about twenty minutes to get to the Basilica, possibly less as there was no real traffic on the roads because of the virus. He was my only hope.

About twenty other men in black suits soon joined the search around the Plaza and the Basilicas. Speaking to one another, they split into small groups and started randomly searching for me in the trees, behind the walls, in the gardens, and inside the Basilicas.

The Swine Flu virus had caused me to almost get killed twice by people I didn't even know. At this moment, I was asking myself only one question: Why on Earth did I get involved in the first place?

As I was trying to get to a better hidden spot, throngs of other questions came to my mind… How did these guys get to know anything about my investigation? How did they know where to find me? What did they think I knew? If they were only following me until now, what could have triggered their sudden intention to kill me? What or who?

Was *DoctorVanity1918* actually a mole? Was she simply one of them? Was she a double agent? Or did our meeting in the Basilica trigger the shooting?

I was well hidden and still keeping an eye on my pursuers when I opened the small blue velvet book with the engraved cross that my contact had given me earlier. I must say that at first, I had thought it was a small Bible in Spanish. It wasn't. It was actually a book written in English. Its title was: *"The Aztlān Project"*.

*"To kill a man is not to protect a doctrine,
but it is to kill a man.
One doesn't prove his faith in burning a man,
but one proves his faith in burning for it."*
– Sebastian Castellio (1515-1563)

CHAPTER 4. THE BOOK

Book [noun] – a written or printed work, or
composition, which is bound together.

(Excerpt from the Storyteller Dictionary)

25. Excerpt from *"The Aztlān Project"*.

CHAPTER 1.

THE SPANISH CONQUEST.

Hernán Cortés de Monroy y Pizarro, born in 1485 in Medellín (Kingdom of Castile, Spain), assisted Diego Velázquez in his conquest of Cuba in 1511 and received a large estate of land, Indian slaves, mines, and cattle for his efforts. In 1518, he persuaded the newly appointed Governor Velázquez to make him commander of an expedition to establish a colony on the mainland, rumoured to contain great wealth. This place is what we know today as Mexico. Cortés gathered eleven ships and more than six hundred men.

Velázquez, suspicious of Cortés' real motives, decided to cancel the expedition, but Cortés set sail anyway. He and his men landed in Mayan territory. They settled and made local alliances with a few tribes. There, he met Gerónimo de Aguilar, a Franciscan priest who had survived a shipwreck. In March 1519, Cortés formally claimed the land for the Kingdom of Castile, Aragon, and the Empire of Charles V.

He then won a battle in Tabasco against natives, who gave him twenty indigenous women. Among them was a woman called *La Malinche*, his future mistress and mother of his child, who knew both Mexica and Mayan languages. She became a very valuable interpreter for him and with her help, Cortés learned from the Tabascans about the wealthy Mexica Empire, led by Emperor *Motecuhzoma Xocoyotzin*, also known as *Motecuhzoma II*, *Motecuhzoma*, *Montezuma* or *Moctezuma*.

26. The interpreter.

12.04 p.m.

I started to wonder what was taking Pedro so long to get to the Basilicas. I had called him more than twenty minutes before. Where was he? When I tried to call his mobile phone again, I ended up talking to his answering machine. I was getting worried. What was going on?

Since I had Pedro's girlfriend's fixed number in case of emergency, I called her too. Mary was Irish.

'Mary? This is Jean-Baptiste calling. How are you doing?'

'Oh hello, Jean-Baptiste. I'm fine and you?'

'I was just wondering if Pedro left the house a while ago, because I'm at the Basilica de Guadalupe in Mexico City waiting for him, and he doesn't seem to be around…'

'Well, I saw him leaving the house at about twenty or quarter to twelve…' she replied calmly. 'Anyway, he always carries his mobile with him and always answers, so you might want to try and call him.'

Mary, originally from a seaside town about twenty kilometres south of Dublin called Bray, was normally of a very placid nature. I actually knew her before knowing Pedro. We had met a couple of times in London after the 2005 coordinated suicide attacks on the city's public transport system, as she was working for the Greater London Authority at the time.

'That's the problem, Mary… I called him twice already and each time I just get his answering machine!' I explained while anxiously keeping an eye on the bald men who were still trying to find me. 'He's not answering the phone!'

'What answering machine are you talking about?' Mary asked, suddenly filled with apprehension. 'Jean-Baptiste, he has never set any answering machine… he doesn't know how to set it up!'

That was really worrying.

'Mary, don't panic, I'm sure there's a good explanation behind all this. Let me call you as soon as I meet him, ok?' I told her, trying to convince her that nothing had happened to Pedro.

But was I trying to convince her or myself? I now suspected that something really bad had happened to Pedro, but I didn't know what exactly. He was more than my interpreter, he was my friend. He was my only way to communicate with people in this country.

Damned answering machine!

27. Excerpt from *"The Aztlān Project"*.

CHAPTER 2.

CORTÉS AND THE HANDLING OF CHOLULA.

In July 1519, Cortés took over Veracruz and placed himself directly under the orders of King Charles V. There, he met some of the Mexica ruler's tributaries; he asked them to arrange a meeting with Moctezuma II, who turned down every meeting. Cortés was determined to meet with him and left Veracruz to march on Tenochtitlán, along with about four hundred men and hundreds of indigenous carriers and warriors.

As a matter of fact, since 1517, Moctezuma II was already receiving reports of Europeans landing on the east coast of the Mexica Empire. Moctezuma II ordered that he was kept informed of any new such sightings. So when Cortés arrived in 1519, Moctezuma II was aware of the Spanish presence and he decided to send emissaries to meet them.

During his journey to Tenochtitlán, Cortés made some important alliances with some native tribes such as the Nahuas of Tlaxcala, the Tlaxcalans, and the Totonacs. In October 1519, Cortés and his men, accompanied by about 3,000 Tlaxcalans, marched to Cholula, the second largest city in central Mexico. In a pre-meditated effort to inspire fear on the Mexica who were waiting for him in the capital of the Empire, Cortés organised the planned massacre of thousands of unarmed members of the nobility, all gathered at the central Plaza of Cholula, before partially burning the great city.

28. The Plaza.

12.13 p.m.

I couldn't wait any longer. I wanted and needed to leave this place discreetly, even though the bald men were still looking for me… So I decided to send an SMS to Carlos Thomson, a friend at my hotel. He was a Mexican journalist who I had worked with on several occasions, on various stories, including one on Cuba's Guantanamo Bay, about five years ago.

J.B.: Hi Carlos. Are u busy right now? Need ur help urgently!

Carlos: Hi JB. Am at hotel. What's happened?

J.B.: Can't say anything by SMS… too long to explain. Can we meet?

Carlos: Sure. Where are u?

J.B.: Basilica de Guadalupe. Where can I find u?

Carlos: Let's meet at entrance of supermarket Mega, on Calzada Ticoman.

J.B.: Ok, I'll find it with my GPS. Can't wait to see u!

Carlos: Hope u are ok. I'll be there in about 15 min.

J.B.: Tks. See u there then!

After checking the supermarket's location on my iPhone GPS application, I saw that it was approximately a five minute-walk from my location. That wasn't too far.

Suddenly, I noticed that six of the men in black were slowly making their way to the Plaza, tightly holding someone. Even though I was quite a distance from them, I immediately recognised their prisoner as Pedro.

They made him talk through a loudspeaker.

'Señor Duprés, please, you must surrender now! Otherwise they will kill me!'

That was a difficult situation. If I surrendered now, they would certainly kill me. However, they would also definitely kill him anyway. They wouldn't let him live after what he had probably seen and heard… I didn't know what to do. I couldn't just walk away and let him die. Or could I?

I made up my mind and decided to run away. I stood up from my hideout and ran as fast as I could on the roof of the Basilica. Fortunately, the sprain on my left foot wasn't too bad to prevent me from running. Someone must have seen me leaving because all of a sudden, people started shouting in Spanish everywhere. Then I heard two gunshots behind me, and another one, and again, and again…

I was still running on the roof and didn't want to look at what was happening behind me. I had to get away quickly. I jumped from the roof onto the top of a small wooden booth, which I literally smashed with my fall. A private guard, who had been happily watching something on TV, managed to jump out of the booth just in time to avoid being injured. He obviously went crazy when he noticed I had just shattered his TV.

I had no time to waste with him, and I couldn't speak Spanish anyway, so I started running again. But now the sprain was hurting again, probably because of the fall. As I limped through the gate, everything around me went silent. Then seven birds rose in the blue sky one at a time, flying away from a tree situated before the Basilica's gate.

I heard a loud gunshot. Only one thought came to my mind: they had just killed Pedro. Right there, in front of the Basilicas, in the middle of the Plaza.

29. Excerpt from *"The Aztlān Project"*.

CHAPTER 3.

MISUNDERSTANDING.

On 8th November 1519, after a three-month journey, Hernán Cortés eventually arrived in what he called *"The City of Gold"*, Tenochtitlán. He was peacefully received by the Mexica Emperor Moctezuma II, who even gave him and his men sumptuous gifts made of gold. Moctezuma II gave Cortés the gift of a Mexica calendar and two discs made of gold and silver; gifts that Cortés later melted for their value. Of all the cities in Europe, probably only Constantinople was larger than Tenochtitlán.

In his letters to King Charles V, Cortés claimed to have learned that the arrival of the Spanish coincided with a Mexica prophecy about a white-skinned god coming from the east. He thought he had been mistaken and was being considered by the Mexica to be the feathered serpent god Quetzalcoatl. But Cortés had been misled somewhat by his close friend, Father Gerónimo de Aguilar, who at the time was holding millenarian beliefs. He had inaccurately told Cortés about the Mexica prophecy. If the idea of the natives taking the Spanish conquerors for gods was perfect for Cortés and his men, an ideal fantasy, it was actually a total misunderstanding.

The prophecy did exist, but the Mexica knew from the beginning that the Spaniards weren't gods at all. At first, Moctezuma II offered them golden gifts to be polite and keep them away from his Empire, but as Cortés insisted on meeting with him, and he hungered for gold, the Mexica Emperor then deliberately led the Spanish man into the heart of the Mexica Empire. He brought him to his palace, where the Spaniards lived as his guests for several months, with the hope of getting to know Cortés' weaknesses, study his behaviour, learn his strategies, and crush him later. Moctezuma II continued governing his empire and even undertook conquests of new territory while Cortés stayed in Tenochtitlán.

The relationship between the two men which, at first, was one of courtesy, very quickly deteriorated when the Mexica nobility became increasingly annoyed with the presence of the large Spanish army in the capital and more specifically, the Tlaxcalans, the Mexica's enemies. Moctezuma II eventually told Cortés that he needed to leave Tenochtitlán. But Cortés didn't want to leave.

30. Nobleness.

12.20 p.m.

After running a little bit through the small streets of the neighbourhood, I finally made it to the supermarket. There, I heard a loud vehicle horn in the vast car park. I looked around and spotted Carlos at the wheel of a silver Seat Córdoba.

I was so afraid that the men in black were running after me that I almost jumped into his car. I hid behind Carlos' seat with a brown blanket that I found on the passenger's seats covering my body.

It was so hot in this car. There was absolutely no wind. It felt like 50° Celsius under the blanket. I asked Carlos to start driving so that nobody could catch us.

Carlos was a pleasant fellow who I had worked with a few times in Cuba. He was a bit fat, with long curly hair, and a long curly beard. He was wearing yellow glasses and a flowery blue and pink t-shirt. His English was really good and his Spanish accent was very subtle. He wasn't wearing any mask.

Hidden and in the dark, I received an SMS on my iPhone. It was my fiancée, Sarah.

Sarah: Hello Mister! Just to know if ur ok there?

J.B.: Am ok. What about u?

Sarah: Ok too. Even if 2 cases of Sw-F have just been confirmed in Scotland.

J.B.: Wow. That's close to u. Please take care and let me know.

Sarah: I miss u a lot, JB!

J.B.: Miss u too. Je t'aime.

Sarah : Je t'aime.

I had been living in London since 1994, when I moved from Paris. During my stay in Mexico, Sarah was working there. I knew she was a bit scared being alone with all the media frenzy around the Swine Flu, and I felt slightly useless being so far from her. But I had to be strong and get on with my work.

The car stopped. Carlos reassured me it was just the traffic lights. He also told me that 149 people had now died of the suspected Swine Flu virus in Mexico, all aged between 20 and 50 years old. Then he asked me what was going on and who exactly was after me. I explained everything in detail, from the improvised meeting at the laboratory to the men in black at the Basilicas.

'I must say I find it hard to believe anyone would chase you and try to kill you simply because of the Swine Flu virus. I'd understand someone trying to kill you if you were about to find out who was behind the Swine Flu story, but it's obviously not the case!'

I realised I had forgotten to tell him about my secret contact and our meeting at the Basilica, but before I could tell him, Carlos asked me if I would agree to meet someone he knew in the capital who could help me with my investigation. I took the blanket off and sat by his side. I looked at him, smiling at his funny glasses and I agreed.

Carlos told me that an earthquake had hit Mexico City earlier, with a magnitude 5.6 on the Richter scale. I had felt some vibrations at the Basilica actually. He drove me south of the city to the Cuauhtémoc borough of Mexico City to a square named Plaza de las Tres Culturas. It was surrounded by an excavated Mexica archaeological site, an old church, a massive housing complex, and some office complexes.

We left the car and made our way to the centre of the park. There stood the *Templo de Santiago*, a baroque-style church. It was a very old, dark, and shady-looking church. It also came across as being quite uninteresting and uninviting. As we passed the Mexica ruins, Carlos started telling me a bit about its history.

'This church was built at the beginning of the seventeenth century on the site of a small chapel of 1535. That chapel belonged to the Franciscan convent of Santiago. Attached to the church is one of the oldest conventional buildings in America, formerly called *Colegio Imperial de Santa Cruz*. It was there that the Franciscans taught the sons of the Mexica nobility, after the fall of their Empire.'

'Why the sons of the Mexica nobility?'

'The school's objective was to educate an indigenous priesthood so its pupils were selected from the most prestigious families of the former Mexica ruling class. They were taught in Spanish, Latin, and Greek, but also in Nahuatl, the language of the Mexica, which has been spoken in Central Mexico since at least the seventh century.'

I stopped Carlos in front of the wooden doors as he was about to enter the church.

'How do you know all this?'

'Twenty years ago, I studied at the University of Cantabria, in Spain,' Carlos explained. 'There was a course of ethnography where I learnt a lot about one of the most remarkable teachers of that Mexican school. His name was Bernardino de Sahagún and he was the greatest chronicler of the history of New Spain. With the help of his trilingual Mexica students, he managed to extract some important information from the elders about the history and culture of the Mexica and the late Empire, before transcribing everything in Spanish as well as in Nahuatl.'

31. Breaking News.

24WNN, USA.

New cases of Swine Flu were confirmed on Monday in the United States (47), Mexico (26), Canada (6), Scotland (2) and Spain (1). The virus is now believed to be responsible for at least 149 deaths in Mexico, while 2,000 have been hospitalized.

The World Health Organization has now raised its pandemic alert level to four, indicating that the UN body has determined, "The virus is capable of significant human-to-human transmission."

U.S. President Barack Obama said on Monday that the outbreak was "a cause for concern but not a cause for alarm." He also said that the federal government was "closely monitoring emerging cases and had declared a public health emergency as a precautionary tool to ensure the availability of adequate resources to combat the spread of the virus."

32. Excerpt from *"The Aztlān Project"*.

CHAPTER 4.

HOW THE TENSION ENDED UP IN A REVOLT...

In April 1520, Governor Velázquez sent an expedition to capture Hernán Cortés to punish his mutiny. As he left the city to fight the Spanish expedition, a Mexica revolt began in Tenochtitlán because of a massacre in the main temple of the city. This turned the already difficult situation between the Spaniards and the Mexica into direct violence.

Cortés won the battle without even needing the extra troops as reinforcements against the Mexica. On his return, Cortés ordered Moctezuma II to be kept prisoner in his own palace. He became a hostage used by the Spaniards to assure their security against any Mexica revolt. Cortés also ordered him to swear allegiance to Charles V and to convert to Christianism. Then Cortés obliged Moctezuma II to face the crowd from the balcony of his palace on 29th June 1520, where he had to demand all the gold of the empire be brought to the palace so he could be freed by the Spaniards. The gold was duly delivered, but Moctezuma II remained prisoner.

Knowing that their leader was still captive and having to feed the Spaniards as well as thousands of their enemies, the residents of Tenochtitlán began to feel the burden on their shoulders; they resorted to rioting in the streets. Cortés ordered Moctezuma II to ask his people to stop fighting. The Mexica ruler told him that at that point they would not listen to him; he suggested Cortés free his young brother, Cuitlahuac, so that he could convince them to dispose of their arms and not fight anymore.

Cortés freed Cuitlahuac. However once he was free, Cuitlahuac led his people against the Conquistadors. Feeling totally betrayed by him, Cortés, in a highly desperate and elaborate action, personally poured molten gold down Moctezuma's throat, simultaneously drowning, suffocating, and burning him to death.

33. Darkness.

12.58 p.m.

As we entered the church, Carlos whispered in my ear, asking me to have a seat on a pew on the first row of the nave, while he was going to look for his friend, who he wanted to introduce me to. Then he vanished through a door somewhere behind the altar, leaving me alone in the church.

There were almost no lights inside the church, just a few candles flickering in front of a broken statue of Saint James, one of the twelve apostles of Jesus Christ. It was strangely as cold inside the church as it was hot outside…

With only my t-shirt and jeans, I felt like I was in a fridge. It was even colder than what I had experienced during some of my winter holidays in Canada. I thought that this was probably what it felt like to be dead. That really was the weirdest sensation ever.

Waiting for Carlos in the freezing cold and sitting alone in the dark, I thought over everything that had happened since I started this investigation. It began with a virus spreading around the world, then I got involved, met an enigmatic professor at a laboratory, met my mysterious contact in a basilica, then got chased by strange bald men who had tried to kill me, before they executed Pedro… Maybe I was now going to write another chapter of this story by meeting yet another mysterious person. My life sounded a bit like a fiction novel right now, and I sincerely wished it was one…

By my side, on the pew was a small flyer with a picture of the church. It was a leaflet referring to the *Tlatelolco massacre*, which was a government massacre of student and civilian protesters that took place in 1968, just ten days before the Summer Olympics, in Mexico City… in this very *Plaza de las Tres Culturas*. It was explained that the estimates placed the death toll between two and three hundred deaths, with over a thousand arrests. At the time, the Mexican government propaganda and the media of the country claimed that government forces had been provoked by students shooting at them, but official documents were now showing that the snipers who triggered the massacre were in fact members of the Presidential Guard.

Terrifying!

34. Excerpt from *"The Aztlān Project"*.

CHAPTER 5.

THE TLAXCALANS SEALED THEIR FATE.

Incurring heavy losses, Cortés and his men were driven out of the city on 30th June 1520. After having ruled for just 80 days, Cuitlahuac soon died of smallpox, one of the diseases that had unfortunately been involuntary introduced to the New World by the Spanish.

The Spaniards took refuge in Tlaxcala, and signed a treaty with the Tlaxcalans to conquer Tenochtitlán, offering them freedom from any tribute and the control of Tenochtitlán after the battle. In the meantime, the Mexica chose a new ruler, Cuauhtémoc, a nephew of Moctezuma II. The Mexica sent emissaries to ask the Tlaxcalans to turn the Spaniards over to them, but the people of Tlaxcala were resolute and categorically refused.

35. Breaking News.

The Impartial Newspaper, UK.

Felipe Solis, the renown Mexican archaeologist who guided President Barack Obama around Mexico City's anthropology museum during his visit to Mexico earlier this month, died the next day from "flu-like symptoms". Mr Obama, who later attended the Americas summit in Trinidad and Tobago, met Mr Solis at a gala dinner held at the museum, on 16 April.

36. Carlos' friend.

1.08 p.m.

Carlos reappeared from the door behind the altar. Somebody else was with him too. It was a priest dressed in a black cassock, a long close-fitting, ankle-length robe, but without any clerical collar.

I couldn't see his face in the dark. Carlos prompted me to follow him to an old confessional where I would be speaking to him. The priest entered one compartment, I entered the other. We were only separated by a thick wooden lattice. There was also a crucifix hanging just over me.

I had no option but to kneel on the wooden kneeler built into the walls of the confessional, as any penitent would, to converse with the priest. That was a slightly uncomfortable position, I have to say.

When I was ready, the door of my compartment got locked and the priest glided the sliding screen so that he could address me; I wouldn't be able to see his face. He quickly started the conversation in a whisper and in perfect English.

'I knew that you were going to come and see me at some point, Mister Duprés,' he announced before adding, 'I am sure you would like to know why I knew we would meet.'

I was baffled.

'Who are you?'

'Let's just say that I am a senior member of a private organisation here in Mexico City called *The Aztlān Project.*'

I knew that name… *The Aztlān Project* was the title of that little blue book my contact had given me at the Basilica.

'*Aztlān* members are always very secretive and distrustful. So you will understand that I prefer you do not see my face for this first meeting,' the priest explained.

'Oh… you mean that we will definitely meet again?'

'We will, Mister Duprés, and after what you will soon discover, I think you will certainly want to meet me again. But let me first come to the subject of your visit today: the Swine Flu virus!'

I couldn't believe it. I felt like I was being directed by someone. Did these people know me so well that they could even decide my own thoughts?

'Our members believe that the virus may be a biological weapon that went totally wrong…'

'How can you prove that?' I asked doubtfully.

'Did you know that sixteen eminent microbiologists, leaders in their field of scientific research, either died or went missing in the last eight weeks?' he answered slowly in a low-pitched voice. 'I mean international microbiologists, not only Mexicans or Americans. These people were specialised in biological agents, DNA sequencing, and more importantly… infectious diseases!'

Silence.

'We believe that somebody has decided to get rid of infectious disease researchers with only one purpose…'

'Hum… there would really be only one reason to kill this bunch of scientists…' I added. 'To keep them from doing something they are able to do.'

'Exactly. Like speak up if an artificially created disease is being used through the mutation of a natural one.'

I was confused. Had the Swine Flu virus really been created to kill or did it really have natural beginnings?

'The virus has been described everywhere as a completely new strain of the H1N1 virus, as a mix of human-avian-swine viruses. But a very interesting question is: has there been any reported A-H1N1 infections of pigs or birds until now? The not so interesting answer is: no!'

37. Excerpt from *"The Aztlān Project"*.

CHAPTER 6.

THE END OF THE MEXICA EMPIRE.

After reorganising his army and getting some reinforcements from Cuba, Cortés returned to Tenochtitlán in 1521 to cut off all supplies to the island city. Tenochtitlán fell after a three-month siege and the Spanish slaughtered nearly half of the city's population.

On 13th August 1521, the Mexica Empire totally disappeared and Cortés was able to claim it for Spain. A new settlement, Mexico City, was immediately built on the ruins of the Mexica capital, with Spanish colonists. Cortés secured control over Mexico and ordered extreme acts of cruelty on the indigenous population. Western diseases such as smallpox, measles, and mumps killed the survivors. In the siege of Tenochtitlán, about 240,000 Mexica died. Finally, to eradicate the remaining Mexica, the conquerors took Mexica women as wives and mistresses, creating half-breed *"mestizos".* They used the men as slaves.

From 1521 to 1524, Cortés governed Mexico personally. In 1523, he was named Governor and Captain General of New Spain by Charles V. He was one of the first to import African slaves to Mexico. In 1528, fearing that he was becoming too powerful, the King forced Cortés to return to Spain where he was reinstated as Captain General. Back in Mexico, his powers were limited and his activities monitored.

In 1541, Cortés returned to Spain an embittered man. He retired to an estate near Seville where he died on 2nd December 1547.

CHAPTER 7.

ASSIMILATION AND INDOCTRINATION.

Unfortunately for the Tlaxcalans, and contrary to their belief, the Spanish never had the intention of turning the city of Tenochtitlán over to them. While Tlaxcalans troops continued to help the Spaniards after the fall of Tenochtitlán, the Spanish would be the new rulers and would eventually disown the treaty with the Tlaxcalans.

The Conquistadors kept a part of their promise: Tlaxcala wasn't destroyed after the conquest and Tlaxcalans were allowed to keep their indigenous names. However, forty years after the conquest, the Tlaxcalans had to pay the same tributes as any of the other indigenous cultures in Mexico. Their trust had been totally misplaced.

As for the Mexica, their education system was abolished and replaced by a very limited church education. Even foods associated with Mesoamerican religious practices were forbidden. Eventually, the natives were forbidden to learn about their cultures and even to learn to read and write in Spanish. In some areas, they would be declared minors, forbidden to learn to read and write at all, so they would always need a Spanish man in charge of them to be responsible for their indoctrination.

38. Trust no one.

1.27 p.m.

Did the priest want me to buy his story that easily? If that was a joke, I wasn't going to be duped without a hitch. Yes, every government of the planet has lied to their population about something at some time. That's why people always find it difficult to believe in politicians and politics, because of the machinations and manoeuvrings. In a way, that's why it's so much easier to believe in people like the Aztlāns.

But right now, I wanted to know more about their organisation. Who were these people? Why would I trust them in the first place? So I started asking the priest questions.

'How did you come to these conclusions? How do you know all this information about the missing microbiologists? Did you actually know anything about the virus before the outbreak?'

'I cannot tell you anything else for the moment,' the priest answered quickly. 'Trust me, we will meet again soon and then you will get to know a little bit more about us.'

The sliding screen abruptly slipped back to its original position and I heard the priest leaving the confessional at a slow pace. I couldn't run after him since my door was still locked. As I tried and tried to force the lock, the door suddenly opened. It was Carlos.

'Why… why did you lock me in here?' I asked, very upset.

'I didn't,' Carlos answered, before pointing at someone in the dark. 'He did.'

A very tall man appeared in front of me. He was as tall as the confessional. He was also extremely powerfully built, and didn't look too pleased to see my agitated behaviour towards Carlos. I decided to calm down a bit.

'Sergio doesn't speak a word of English, but when someone gets too upset, he also gets upset.'

Sergio, a blond man in his thirties, didn't look like the cleverest man on Earth, but he had some very strong arguments: his muscles and his height. He was dressed as a bouncer and certainly had the charisma that goes with it.

'I want to understand what's going on, Carlos,' I insisted. 'Having people chasing me and then trying to kill me is not something I would define as normal… Where is the priest gone?'

'I can't help you with that right now, I'm sorry,' my Spanish colleague responded. 'No need to even bother trying to find him…'

'Are you yourself a member of this Aztlān organisation?'

'Yes, I am.'

'What is this organisation?'

'Now, as I believe your hotel is under surveillance, it would be stupid to try to get there,' Carlos declared, changing the subject of our conversation. 'So Sergio and I will be taking you to a safe place immediately, somewhere outside the city.'

'Wait! How can I trust you people? You don't even want to explain anything to me about your activities. Really, why would I trust you? How do I know that the men who are after me have not been sent by your friend the priest in order to kill me?'

'It very simple, Jean-Baptiste,' Carlos replied with a smile on his face, 'if we wanted you dead, you wouldn't have had the opportunity to speak to my friend in this confessional!'

Good point. But I still felt like I should trust no one. Nothing was obvious to me anymore. I felt disconnected from reality. My trust had been so badly hurt that I wasn't sure who or what to believe at this point.

39. Excerpt from *"The Aztlān Project"*.

CHAPTER 8.

THE LAST OF THE MEXICA.

A small group of Mexica survivors of the Tenochtitlán massacre hid for years in the region of Honduras with the Lencas, an indigenous people of south-western Honduras, until the Spanish invaded them in 1523. They integrated the Lencas to fight the Conquistadors alongside them. But they were defeated again and again. They returned to the new city of Mexico, where they all acted as any other surviving natives in the city, under the scrutiny of the Spanish.

Nevertheless, they created a small secret committee governed by a *Tlatoani* and seven other members. *Tlatoani* is a Nahuatl term that literally means *speaker*, but may also be translated as *"king"*. The last Tlatoani before the fall of Tenochtitlán was Cuauhtémoc, a nephew of Emperor Moctezuma II, in 1520.

One night in 1524, during the ceremony that founded the secret Mexica council, the newly elected Tlatoani and the seven members of the council took centre stage and swore an oath in front of an audience of probably five hundred people. The oath was they would always fight the Spanish on every land that belonged to their people and they would do everything in their power to one day recreate the lost Mexica Empire with its richness and its culture, as in the legendary ancestral home of Aztlān.

The Tlatoani ripped into *"the endless and brutal Spanish invasion of Mexica territories"* and urged *"all Mexica to reclaim the land of their birth, because the call of their blood is their power, their responsibility, and their inevitable destiny."*

Having understood the importance of gold in the Conquistadors' world, the Tlatoani and the council also pledged to regain possession of all the gold the Spanish had stolen from their Empire. Finally, they vowed to fight until their last breath to see the invaders return to Spain, either dead or alive. The committee agreed that all future new Tlatoani and all new members would have to swear the same oath.

The secret organisation was named after the lost Mexica Empire: *El Proyecto de Aztlān… "The Aztlān Project".*

40. Sacrifices.

2.01 p.m.

Carlos led the way to the exit. The gorilla was following me. The door was wide open and the light coming into the church was like a solace to me. Even though I was still inside the church, the light was already warming me up. My heart started to slow down so my body's temperature didn't overheat me.

Once outside the church, Carlos asked me to hurry to another car that was waiting for us outside the square, to avoid catching the eyes of any men in black that were around. As we made our way out of the church, I saw a huge stele on the Plaza. It was the monument the leaflet said was dedicated to the remembrance of the students killed during the Tlatelolco Massacre of 1968. The names of the people who lost their lives during the event were engraved in 1993, for the 25th anniversary of the terrible events.

Then we passed in front of the Temple of Ehecatl-Quetzalcoatl, a structure with a staircase, a rectangular façade, and a circular body. As we were walking towards the outside of the square, Carlos stopped to explain where we were.

'Between 1987 and 1989, archaeologists uncovered not less than forty-one burials and fifty-four offerings in this temple, including infants in large, wide-mouthed earthenware pots. These were offerings dedicated to Ehecatl, the Mexica god of the winds, who was also another form of the god of the sky, Quetzalcoatl. He could also bring life to all that was lifeless.'

'Infants?' I asked, quite surprised. He didn't answer me, but started walking again. I followed him and we left the archaeological site. We found the car, a crystal black Honda Civic Si Sedán, parked right before the building of the Centro Cultural Universitario Tlatelolco. We jumped in the car, Carlos got in the driver's seat, Sergio sat beside him, while I jumped in the back.

'Are you saying that the Mexica would even kill small children during their rituals of human sacrifices?' I asked Carlos.

'Yes, infant sacrifices,' Carlos answered, starting the car. 'You have to understand that before the Conquistadors, Tlatelolco was certainly the most important commercial centre in Mesoamerica. A lot of trade was happening here. But it was also a place to worship, to entertain, and to play. At that time, human sacrifices weren't seen as the cruel and barbaric act we see it as today. Human sacrifice was a long cultural tradition and the highest level of offerings through which the Mexica sought to repay their debt to the gods.'

'Which debt?'

'In the Mexica's *Legend of the Five Suns*, it is said that there were four suns, one after the other. When the last one died, the gods sacrificed themselves to create a fifth sun, so that mankind could live,' Carlos explained, while driving along the empty streets. 'Therefore, the Mexica believed that their divine duty was to sacrifice themselves and their enemies – usually prisoners of war – in order to provide the sun with his nourishment, which would make the universe survive. Without it, the sun would disappear and the universe would die, and everyone would die too. That's why in their sacrificial hymns, the Mexica described the victims as being *"sent to the gods to plead for us"* or *"consecrated to put an end to all sins"*. Human sacrifice was very much an honour in this sense rather than a sanguinary and murderous practice.'

'Do the members of your Aztlān organisation still practice human sacrifices?' I dared to ask.

The car stopped instantly. While Sergio was peacefully eating some sunflower seeds, Carlos turned to me with an extremely tense look. His eyes were like fire.

'Are you laughing at me now?' he asked, pointing his finger at me. 'What do you think? Because our organisation is secret it means we're the bad guys here? Do you think we are the troublemakers? This isn't the *Da Vinci Code*, my friend! This is real life!'

'I…'

'Who do you think you are, after all?' he continued, raising his voice and getting Sergio's attention. 'You are not the *chosen one* who will discover all the truth about everything and then have some spare time to save the world!'

Sergio had stopped eating his seeds and was staring at me.

'You are just a journalist who decided to get involved in something that he had no clue what it was all about. Because you made it so easy for them to see you coming with your big *gringo* shoes, so easy to find you, now you are their target and of course, *WE* have to save your skin!'

'Well…'

'Let me just tell you one thing: you are not the hero of this story. You are merely a character, and so am I…'

As Carlos started to calm down again, Sergio stopped looking at me and turned his attention to opening another bag of seeds to eat. The car started moving again. Carlos hadn't answered my question at all but had just thrown a lot of anger at me.

This wasn't the man I had worked with in Cuba, a few years ago. This was a very angry man. I didn't know what was driving his anger, but after that conversation, I felt that I was soon going to find out.

41. Excerpt from *"The Aztlān Project"*.

CHAPTER 9.

THE SPANISH HUNGERED FOR GOLD.

The Mexica used to call gold the *"excrement of the gods"* and didn't consider it as particularly precious. Yet it was extremely valuable to the Spanish. When Cortés arrived near Tenochtitlán, Moctezuma II sent many presents to the Spanish. Bernardino de Sahagún, a Spanish Franciscan missionary to the Mexica, best known as the compiler of the *"Florentine Codex"* said:

"They gave the Spanish gold flags, flags of quetzal feathers, and gold necklaces. And when they had given them this, their faces were smiling, they were very glad (the Spaniards), they were delighted. As if they were monkeys they picked up gold, because they seated in such gesture, as if their hearts were renewed and illuminated. Because true it is that is what they yearn for with great thirst. Their chests widen, they are furiously hungry for it. Like hungry pigs they crave gold."

Another example of the Spanish hunger for gold was when Moctezuma II died; instead of administering him the last sacraments, the Spanish priests are said to have been occupied searching for gold in his palace.

After the fall of the Mexica Empire, the Spanish discovered more than eight tons of gold in Mexico, which contributed to about ten percent of the total world production of gold.

42. The hotel.

4.11 p.m.

It took us two hours to finally get to our destination. I stayed quiet for the whole trip, discreetly reading some pages of my little blue book and learning some more things about the Spanish Conquest of Mexico, while sharing a heavy silence with two people who didn't say a word all the way. We stopped at least three times on the way so that Sergio could relieve himself after drinking two 2-litres bottle of Cola that Carlos had bought him at a petrol station outside Mexico City.

Why did I agree to follow Carlos despite the fact his secret organisation didn't seem to want to give me any clue why someone was trying to kill me? Basically, because I couldn't trust anybody else in Mexico City. Not that I would have trusted Carlos with my life, even though I knew him from our work in Cuba, but it would have been foolish of me to try to escape my chasers while not speaking a word of Spanish in a city that I didn't even know. Right now, Carlos was my only way of staying alive.

The car stopped for the last time. We had arrived in one of the oldest cities in Mexico called Tlaxcala, the capital city of the Mexican state of Tlaxcala. My two *friends* escorted me to a small hotel in the city centre called *El espíritu*. When we got to the reception, we didn't stop to check-in. They didn't even speak to the young man who just had a glimpse of them before getting back to his game of solitaire. They simply led the way up a dirty staircase to the first floor, where my room was located. Room number seven. I supposed they had booked the room beforehand.

Carlos opened the door and we entered the small room, one after the other in the dark. Then he opened the long brown curtain to light up the room. There was a bed without a sheet, an old TV, a small closet, and two blue plastic chairs in the room. The shower room was very small too. The room didn't look very clean, but it certainly looked cleaner than the corridor. The door stayed wide open behind us.

'This is your room,' he announced coldly. 'It is paid for, so don't worry about anything other than staying hidden for the moment.'

'Well, that looks to me as if I were your prisoner,' I commented while sitting on the bed. 'You offer me a room that I'm not supposed to move from... Are you going to be next door, spying on me and following my every move within the hotel, around the hotel and outside this city?'

Sergio was looking at the street by the window, his mouth full of cookies, gabbling on in Spanish. Carlos didn't really pay attention to him and answered me instead.

'You are not our prisoner, Jean-Baptiste,' he insisted. 'You are free to go wherever you want, whenever you want. We are just offering you shelter. A place to hide from the people who are after you. If you wish not to accept our hospitality, that's your problem!'

'Why did we have to go so far from Mexico City?'

Silence.

'You might find that Tlaxcala and its surroundings can be an interesting place to stay for a little while…' he answered before calling Sergio and leaving the room.

When he closed the wooden door, I noticed that something was hanging on top of it. It was a small beige envelope attached to the door with a pin. Inside the envelope, I found a folded and ripped piece of newspaper and a small ancient golden key. A name was engraved on the key: *Jean Fleury*. On the newspaper, another name was handwritten in red ink on top of an article in Spanish:

Miguel Serez.

43. Excerpt from *"The Aztlān Project"*.

CHAPTER 10.

ACT OF PIRACY.

In 1522, some of the gold that Cortés and his men had stolen from the Mexica was conveyed to Spain by Cortés' closest friends, the treasurer Julián de Alderete, Captain Antonio Quiñones, and Alonso de Ávila, to keep receiving the King's favour. But on their way to Spain aboard three galleons carrying the Mexica gold for Charles V, they were attacked off the southwest coast of Portugal by a French corsair and naval officer, Jean Fleury, with his five-ship squadron. He chased them and then overtook two of them within a few hours. The treasure and Cortés' report on the conquest of Mexico sailed to Normandy and were later presented to the King of France, Francis I, Charles V's fierce enemy.

The third galleon escaped and hid on Santa Maria Island, in the Azores archipelago until Seville sent two ships to escort it to the continent. When it arrived in Spain, part of the treasure left was confiscated by Juan Rodríguez de Fonseca, Archbishop of Rossano and President of the Council of the Indies. Most importantly, he was an enemy of Cortés because the Archbishop considered him a traitor who wanted to claim New Spain for himself.

When Cortés received the news, he was fuming at the act of piracy from the French. He believed that someone had informed Fleury and the French that the three ships would transport gold from Mexico and even what route they would use. But the truth is that Fleury didn't actually know himself that he was attacking ships from the New World.

44. The puzzle.

4.42 p.m.

Miguel Serez, Jean Fleury. What did these two names have to do with my investigation? One of them did ring a bell though. Thanks to my little blue book, I already knew who Jean Fleury was. But who was Miguel Serez?

I was left in my room with a stained carpet on the floor, a damp ceiling, a piece of newspaper, and a small old key. At least the temperature in the room was nice and cool thanks to the very noisy air-conditioning unit.

All these adventures had made me hungry. I hadn't had anything for lunch and I definitely needed to eat something for dinner. But there was no mini-bar and no food to eat in the room.

I decided to leave my room and make my way to the closest restaurant. Passing the reception of the hotel, I noticed that a newspaper had been left on the floor by the reception desk. It had obviously fallen off the desk, I thought. I bent down to pick it up and, as I was about to give it to the young man playing solitaire, I realised that the font used on the newspaper was the same as the one on the paper in my room.

Leaving the reception with the newspaper tucked under my arm, I went to sit on a white plastic bench on the terrace. I took the small envelope from my jeans and tried to compare the fonts. They were identical.

When I turned the front-page of *El Sol de Tlaxcala*, I found an article entitled: *"Desde el 2 de abril advirtieron sobre influenza en granjas"*. With the word *"influenza"* in it, I immediately understood that it was talking about the virus. But more importantly, a piece of the article had been torn out and I had the missing piece. With a mysterious name written on it in red.

Whoever had taken the trouble to put the envelope in my room had probably not realised they were giving me an enormous hint by leaving the newspaper easily available to me at the reception of the hotel. Was it Carlos? Or was it someone else? Despite the fact Carlos had told me I would be absolutely safe here, who else beside him actually knew that I was going to be staying at this hotel, in that room?

45. Excerpt from *"The Aztlān Project"*.

CHAPTER 11.

THE SUBTERFUGE.

In 1523, Charles V, influenced by Bishop Fonseca, sent a military force to conquer and settle the northern part of Mexico. Hernán Cortés mentioned it in his fourth letter to the King, in which he described himself as the victim of a conspiracy by his enemies, Diego Velázquez, Diego Columbus, and Bishop Fonseca. So, in order to win back the King's favours, Cortés outlined a plan that he thought would ensure the gold of the Mexica would not be plundered by pirates on its way to Spain.

Cortés had indeed become so paranoid that he had decided to adopt a subterfuge in response to the attack by the French privateer, Jean Fleury. In any future expedition, the treasure fleets would constitute three galleons to transport the gold from Veracruz to Puerto Rico. They would then make a rendezvous with two convoys from Seville and return together to Spain. They would first head to Oran on the Mediterranean coast, in north-western Algeria. From there, another three armed escorts would join the fleet and take the precious yellow metal to Alicante, a seaport of south-eastern Spain. It would finally be taken by road to reach its final destination, Jaca, a fortified city of north-eastern Spain.

The procedure was established after the recommendations of Pedro de Alvarado, chief lieutenant and second-in-command in the expedition for the conquest of Mexico, and a personal adviser of Cortés.

Cortés had chosen Jaca to guard the treasure because Charles V was the first king to reign in his own right over both the Kingdom of Castile and the Kingdom of Aragon, and the ruler of the Holy Roman Empire. Jaca had the particularity of being the former capital of Aragon and an Episcopal seat with a cathedral that was one of the oldest Romanesque churches in Spain.

Thus, Cortés wanted Saint-Peter's Cathedral of Jaca to secretly shelter the gold of the Mexica.

In his letter, Cortés also explained to Charles V that his subterfuge was of avoiding any new pirate attacks, preventing the King of France from finding the treasure, and preventing the Mexica survivors to ever rebuild their Empire with the gold.

After reading Cortés' letter, the King accepted the conqueror's appeal and sent out a decree forbidding anyone to interfere in the politics of New Spain. Through a secret royal decree, Charles V ordered that all the gold from Mexico be discreetly taken to Jaca by a secret royal military unit, from its arrival in Alicante every month.

46. More questions.

6.09 p.m.

Back from a small restaurant where I ate a *pollo con mole verde,* which I understood to be a chicken in green mole, I was too tired to think any longer. It had been a hell of a day.

I had lost my car, my laptop, my bag and my hotel room in Mexico City. But I still had the two most important things with me, my iPhone and the little blue book. My iPhone was the best way for me to stay in contact, but also to browse the Internet for more information about the Swine Flu virus. I now wanted to find more details about the Aztlān organisation.

As I was reading the very interesting and intriguing story of the book, I was wondering who had actually written it. Was *DoctorVanity1918* the author of the book herself? Who was she really? Why on Earth had she given me that book? Were the men in black after me because of the contents of that book? Why was everyone wearing a mask in Mexico City and in Tlaxcala, except the men in black, the Aztlān members, and the receptionist of this hotel?

I felt I was becoming paranoid with all these questions in my head. So many questions and no real answers until now… The only thing I knew for certain was that I had to keep this book with me as it could contain some crucial information for my investigation.

What about my friend Pedro? He had lost his life because of me. I was feeling guilty for his death. But what if I had surrendered to the men in black at the Basilicas? Would they have killed me only or would they have killed Pedro anyway?

What if we were both dead by now? Then nobody would ever know anything about my findings or my theories… Nobody would ever know anything about what was going on here. I felt it was my duty to stay alive to testify when the time came. It was far beyond my duty as a journalist now. I had to make sure those people responsible for the outbreak of Swine Flu wouldn't win. I had to fight for the truth.

My iPhone was displaying the low-battery sign and I was also in low-battery mode. I needed a good sleep to digest everything that had happened today. I found some clean sheets for my bed in a small closet. I went to bed quite early to get ready for what I could only assume would be yet another day of adventures.

Why did I decide to cancel my previous investigation for this Swine Flu one? Why did I always have to get involved?

47. Excerpt from *"The Aztlān Project"*.

CHAPTER 12.

THE SWISS GUARD.

In December 1523, Pope Clement VII had just been elected and he was worried about the growing power of the Spanish King in Italy. However, he agreed with Charles V to the deployment of a Swiss Guard unit of twenty-two men to look after the cathedral of Jaca.

Charles V had purposely misled him by saying that the cathedral was the most sacred church in Spain and under the threat of a great conspiracy planned by the Sultan of the Ottoman Empire, Suleiman I. Once the Swiss Guard was in place, the soldiers were told that their duty was to protect the *"heart of the Church of Spain"* in the hidden crypt of the cathedral without any details to what this *heart* really was.

Then every month at the same time, freight was delivered to the cathedral by a Spanish military unit. That was the only time of the month when the Swiss Guard was asked to leave the crypt without asking any questions.

Until one day, a Swiss soldier, who was late for his change of duties, fortuitously discovered that the Spanish were actually bringing a real treasure of gold articles inside the crypt, including ingots, small figures, spools, jewellery nose pieces, masks, discs, and other precious items.

He shared his secret with only two of his comrades and on 12th July 1529, they managed to run away from the cathedral with two big bags of gold each, without being noticed by the other guards. They were found dead two days later, slaughtered and hanging on a tree by a ditch on a road outside the city. But the gold was never found.

"Reading is a conversation.
All books talk.
But a good book listens as well."
– Mark Haddon

CHAPTER 5. SECRET & PROJECT

Secret [noun] – confidential or classified information, or knowledge, that is kept or that must be kept hidden.

(Excerpt from the Storyteller Dictionary)

48. Aztlān.

Day 4 – 28th April 2009, 7.30 a.m.

I woke up this morning with one thought. I didn't know much about the Aztlān people after all. So I had to do some research on the Internet. When I googled the words *"Aztlān Project"* on my iPhone, I found many websites talking about the Aztlān legend, the Aztecs, the Mexica, etc.

Aztlān was the legendary ancestral home of the Nahua peoples, a place described by ancient legends as a real paradise. *"Aztec"* was actually the Nahuatl word for *"people from Aztlān"*.

I also found news websites describing the organisation as a secret network that aimed to recreate the ancient Mexica Empire in the valley of Mexico. They were also in favour of achieving *social liberation*, Mexican-American empowerment, and they proposed a new nation be created, the

Republic of Aztlān, an independent nation from the current Mexican republic.

What else did I find out about *The Aztlān Project*? In March 1969, *El Plan de Aztlān*, a clear statement of the growing nationalist consciousness of the Mexica people, was adopted at the first National Chicano Youth Liberation Conference in Denver, Colorado. There, for the first time, the concept of Aztlān, as a nation, was raised. In order to achieve self-determination, said the plan, they needed an independent political party with Mexica nationalism as its common denominator. It was also very important to build relationships and challenge people to act on their faith and values to create a healthy Mexica nation through education and community development.

```
La Voz de Aztlān,
Extract of « El Plan de Aztlāns ».
```

In the spirit of a new people that is conscious not only of its proud historical heritage but also of the brutal "gringo" invasion of our territories, we, the Chicano inhabitants and civilizers of the northern land of Aztlān from whence came our forefathers, reclaiming the land of their birth and consecrating the determination of our people of the sun, declare that the call of our blood is our power, our responsibility, and our inevitable destiny.

Aztlān belongs to those who plant the seeds, water the fields, and gather the crops and not to the foreign Europeans. We do not recognize capricious frontiers on the bronze continent. With our heart in our hands and our hands in the soil, we declare the independence of our nation. We are a bronze people with a bronze culture. Before the world, before all of North America, before all our brothers in the bronze continent, we are a nation, we are a union of free pueblos, we are Aztlān.

As far as I understood it, the Mexica had a lot of resentment towards the Spanish descendants in Mexico, due to all the cruelties, brutalities, and the enslavement their own ancestors had suffered. Could that be another clue? If the organisation was holding such extreme political views against the Spanish descendants in this country, could they get really radical and end up trying to do something to harm them?

The city of Tlaxcala was settled by natives, the Tlaxcalans. During the Spanish Conquest, they had built an alliance with Hernán Cortés against their enemies: the Mexica. Apart from the Spanish themselves, the Tlaxcalans were the only winners of the conquest, while the Mexica were the biggest losers.

Finally among my findings, a very interesting piece of information: it seemed that among the members of the Aztlān organisation, one could count Mexican writers, artists, teachers, intellectuals, and scientists!

What if the Aztlān Project had decided to avenge their ancestors with a virus for example? Having scientists amongst their members, they could have used new technologies to make that possible today. I imagined that if the Aztlāns had the capacity of creating some kind of genetically modified virus that could target only a particular part of the population, they would be successful in their enterprise and get rid of their former enemies.

Would it be possible for scientists to create a virus that would genetically target one particular part of a population, i.e. only react with people who carried certain genes, but not the rest of the population?

What was the easiest way to spread such a lethal virus within the population? Influenza! Influenza could be transmitted by coughs, sneezes, saliva, nasal secretions, blood, through contact with these body fluids or with contaminated surfaces, and also from infected mammals... Moreover, according to the data I had found online, the first people suffering and dying from the Swine Flu virus were surprisingly located in the city of Tlaxcala!

I suddenly had a horrific vision of a virus that was currently killing people around Mexico and that could have been designed by the secret members of the Aztlān Project. The Tlaxcalans' descendants were infected and killed by the virus, while anyone else was only getting a strong flu.

What a horrific idea. Nobody would ever think that the mysterious organisation could be behind such a terrifying conspiracy. If anyone was to be blamed, everyone would turn to the big vaccine laboratories or the government.

The Swine Flu virus could have been the perfect crime.

49. Excerpt from *"The Aztlān Project"*.

CHAPTER 13.

THE CARDINAL'S APPOINTMENT.

On 2nd September 1530, Charles V ordered the appointment of Cardinal Lorenzo Campeggio, an Italian cardinal and politician, to the Spanish bishopric of Huesca and Jaca. Upset by the treason of the three Swiss soldiers, the King decided that at all times, someone would have to account for whatever happened to the treasure. Campeggio held the position until 1534, when he became Bishop of Candia in Crete.

Even though he had lost all his possessions during the sacking of Rome in 1527, which was carried out by the troops of Charles V, Campeggio ultimately accepted the bishopric of Huesca and Jaca because the Spanish King was offering him a great income and the bishopric of Mallorca as compensation for his loss.

Lorenzo Campeggio, who was also the Cardinal Protector of the Holy Roman Empire and the last Cardinal Protector of England, became a close friend of Charles V. He advised him to make Pope Clement VII aware of the existence of the treasure, so that the Vatican would always provide new specialised and professional soldiers for the Swiss Guard in the crypt.

Campeggio finally established the modus operandi, agreed with the Pope, of the appointment of future Cardinals to the Cathedral of Jaca to look after the treasure: every twenty-two years, on the second day of September, the Pope was to appoint a new Cardinal to the bishopric of Huesca and Jaca, on behalf of the King of Spain. The appointment was to be kept secret by the highest ranks of the *Roman Curia*, the central governing body of the entire Roman Catholic Church and the Pope. The appointment was never to be discussed with anybody foreign to the Vatican, and no information or document was to be withheld within the archives of either the Spanish monarchy or the Vatican.

The Cardinal thus appointed was to secretly hold a non-official, unknown, and undisclosed position at the Cathedral of Jaca, with the Swiss Guard under his orders, and most importantly, be responsible for the hidden treasure before the Pope, and before the King of Spain.

50. American.

9.18 a.m.

After a quick breakfast in a modern café opposite my hotel, I went back to my room. No signs of Carlos or Sergio whatsoever. But as I was pushing the door open, I felt a slight resistance. I pushed even stronger and was surprised to find a new small envelope on the floor, as if someone had passed it underneath while I was out. I opened it and got a folded sheet with an article that seemed to have been printed from the Internet:

The Arlington Post, USA.

"Factory farms with large-scale hog and poultry operations are the source of the Swine Flu," said a Mexican lawmaker in the eastern state of Veracruz. It is an accusation that large-scale swine producers in

Mexico absolutely refute, saying that their animals are healthy, adding that, "It is scientifically not possible for swine to infect people with that virus."

Then at the bottom of the page, there was a handwritten message in red:

Go to Santa Isabel Cholula.

Find Miguel Serez to find the truth about the virus!

The person who left the first envelope on my door was most certainly the same as the one who had left this one. They now were giving me very precise instructions. But why would I follow their instructions in the first place? Were they to be trusted? Were they another whistleblower? What if these messages were sent from Carlos and his organisation to divert my attention from the actual truth?

I wanted to know what was so interesting in Santa Isabel Cholula that my presence there would make a difference to my investigation. I managed to ask the hotel receptionist to call a taxi for me and made my way to the small city located an hour south of Tlaxcala.

What did I know about the Swine Flu? I knew that sufferers complained of symptoms including fever, severe cough and large amounts of phlegm. The illness came on very quickly with high fevers, pain in the muscles and the joints, terrible headaches, some vomiting and diarrhoea.

According to my searches on the Internet, in the town of Santa Isabel Cholula alone, about sixty percent of the population had already experienced the symptoms of the virus with respiratory problems. As about fifty percent of the population were going to Mexico every day to work, it was very likely that this was how the virus spread to the capital where the majority of the cases now existed.

As we were about to arrive in town, my taxi-driver started shouting at me in Spanish, pointing at a huge modern factory farm located at the entrance of Santa Isabel Cholula. I couldn't understand a word that he was saying, but I did see a sign on the road: *"Granja Dodgson"*. By the smell in the air, I could only assume it was a pig farm.

My driver, who was very nice and quiet all the way to Santa Isabel Cholula, kept shouting until we eventually stopped in the town centre. I was wondering what had triggered his behaviour. The farm?

Dirty roads widely outnumbered paved ones in Santa Isabel Cholula. In the small town, I witnessed the same scenes that I had already seen in Mexico City and Tlaxcala, with everyone wearing a mask. I left the taxi with the driver still shouting. I was the only one around without a mask, and for that reason I managed to immediately get people's attention. As I was walking in the streets towards the town hall, about twenty to thirty people started looking at me with worried eyes. Then their worry quickly changed into anger. They also started shouting at me. Their pressure was so intense that I had to leave the pavement and stand on the road. Cars had stopped in the street. Some of them even tried to directly confront me, until a young man stood in their way.

He had brown curly hair, he was in his thirties, and he was wearing a red mask, a red t-shirt, and a pair of jeans. After having a word with them, he turned to me.

'Are you American?' he asked me in his Mexican accent, while keeping everyone a few steps behind him. 'They want to know if you are American.'

'I'm not American, I'm French,' I answered with some kind of confidence. 'Does it make a difference?'

'To them, yes. You see, they thought you were another American coming to town to bring more misery to everyone.'

The young man turned to the people standing right behind him and spoke to them in Spanish. There was a sense of relief among them after his explanation. Then, as they were all getting back to their occupations, I could come back on the pavement and have a word with my Good

Samaritan. He invited me to a small café where we could discuss things more peacefully.

51. Excerpt from *"The Aztlān Project"*.

CHAPTER 14.

"IMPERIUM IN IMPERIO".

Even though he was a good friend of Popes Leo X and Clement VII, and somehow was high profile in the Catholic Church, Cardinal Campeggio had one day said, *"The chief source of all the evils is the Roman Curia"*.

The *Roman Curia* was the administrative apparatus of the Catholic Church. It was comprised of forty-two public dicasteries, or organs of charges... and one non-official.

The highest dicastery of the *Roman Curia* was the *Secretaria Apostolica*, or Secretariat of State, composed of twenty-four secretaries. The dicastery works most closely with the Supreme Pontiff in the exercise of his universal mission. One of the secretaries bore the title of Cardinal Secretary of State and held a position of pre-eminence.

The most unknown dicastery of the *Roman Curia* was the one called *In Pectore*. This was a Latin term that referred to the secret appointment of a Cardinal by the Pope every twenty-two years, on the second day of September, to become responsible for the Spanish bishopric of Huesca and Jaca... therefore responsible for Hernán Cortés' hidden treasure in Jaca, before the Supreme Pontiff.

52. Santa Isabel Cholula.

10.42 a.m.

Sitting at the café, I introduced myself to the young man who had saved me from being lynched earlier. I explained who I was and what I was doing in Mexico. He removed his mask to drink a coffee with me.

'My name is Federico de la Vega,' he told me. 'I'm a law student in Mexico City. I really want to say that I am sorry for the reaction of my people in the street.'

'Don't be sorry. I can only imagine what you all have been going through with this virus. I understand that your town was the first to be touched by the Swine Flu, is that correct?'

'As far as the health experts are concerned, yes. But the outbreak didn't surprise anyone in Santa Isabel Cholula, you know… We all knew that something was going to fall on our heads at some point.'

'What do you mean?' I asked, stupefied by this confession.

'I mean that our community has been trying to get the authorities to do something when we discovered that a strange respiratory disease was affecting many of our people over the past few months. Most of us think that this disease was linked to the pollution coming from the new pig farm outside the town.'

'Granja Dodgson?'

'Exactly.' He smiled. 'It's a subsidiary of the US Company Virginia Foods, nothing less than the world's largest pork producer. I bet you could smell the pigs at the entrance of Santa Isabel Cholula.'

'I did notice their perfume!' I smiled too. 'But the authorities surely sent someone to inspect the farm?'

'After our community leaders got arrested and people speaking out against the Granja Dodgson operations received death threats, local health officials eventually decided to investigate the disease at the end of 2008. Their tests revealed that more than sixty percent of our community was definitely infected by a respiratory disease. But the officials didn't confirm what the disease was. As for Granja Dodgson, they obviously denied any wrongdoing and any connection with its work on the farm.'

'I wouldn't expect any less from them,' I answered, while playing with my coffee spoon.

'Scientists have proven that the proximity of factory pig farms and factory poultry farms always increases the risks of a viral recombination and always increases the risks of the emergence of new virulent flu strains. The example of the pigs held near to chicken farms in Indonesia was a warning. These pigs have high-levels of infection from the deadly Bird Flu virus, H5N1, and scientists have already warned that increasing swine facilities adjacent to avian facilities could promote the evolution of the next pandemics even more.'

'Amazing!'

'What is really amazing is that yesterday, after the federal government officially announced the Swine Flu epidemic, some information in the press revealed that the first case of Swine Flu diagnosed in this country was of a four-year-old boy from Santa Isabel Cholula, on 2nd April 2009. To us all, the government knew all along that the disease that was affecting our community was the Swine Flu virus!'

'A boy, you said?' I asked, trying to find the paper with the name on it. 'What's his name?'

'His name is Miguel Serez. Why?'

53. Excerpt from *"The Aztlān Project"*.

CHAPTER 15.

THE DYING SECRET.

The secret of the hidden treasure was admirably kept for more than four hundred years, shared between the Catholic Church and the Spanish monarchy.

But in 1931, King Alfonso XIII left Spain to live in Rome, after local and municipal elections where republican candidates won the majority of votes. Then in 1939, at the end of the Spanish Civil War, the Republican forces surrendered to the Nationalist forces of General Franco.

Alfonso XIII died in Rome, in 1941, without telling the secret to his son Juan, the Count of Barcelona, who was the father of the current King of Spain. When Alfonso XIII died, Hernán Cortés' secret died with him.

54. The link.

5.13 a.m.

So the Miguel Serez I was looking for was a four-year-old boy! How could a four-year-old lead me to the truth about the Swine Flu virus? I asked my new friend if he could take me to meet the little boy.

'Of course, but why do you want to meet him?' he asked, a bit hesitant. 'His parents regard anyone who wants to examine or interrogate the boy with suspicion, you know?'

'I don't actually know exactly what it is I am looking for. But I think there might be something about him that could really help me with my investigation.'

This small and simple town was far from the troubles of the capital. The people's concerns here had nothing to do with the ones of people in Mexico City.

As I was in the territory of the Aztlāns' former enemies, I asked Federico about the Aztlān Project:

'Would you know a Mexican organisation called *"Aztlān Project"*?'

'Never heard of it,' he answered straightaway, as he finished his coffee. 'What is it?'

'Nothing important,' I answered, pretending that I was looking for some money in my jeans' pockets. 'Shall we go and meet Miguel Serez then?'

'Let's go!'

On the pavement next to the terrace of the café, Federico had parked his motorbike, an old red dual seat Harley-Davidson. He gave me a black helmet similar to his and asked me to sit behind him. I wasn't too confident as I had never ridden on a motorbike before. But there was a first time for everything. Starting with a Harley Davidson was certainly going to be something.

In five minutes we arrived in front of a small house where children wearing masks with funny smiles drawn on were bowling in the middle of the street with a ball made of two or three pairs of socks and about ten one-litre plastic bottles of soda. Federico pointed at one of the children.

'This is Miguel Serez,' he told me, showing me a young child who was wearing his shiny hair combed back with gel and running around as if nothing had ever happened to him. He was, amongst his friends, the only one not wearing a mask. 'The newspapers have been calling him *"Patient zero"* as they say that he was the first to get the virus in the world, but to our community, he was not the source of the outbreak, rather the first person in the world to have survived the virus!'

In an investigation of an epidemic, *"Patient zero"* was the initial source of a disease in a population and the possible spread of that disease.

'May I speak to his parents?' I requested, as my driver parked his motorbike by the gate of the house.

'Let's ask him.'

Federico and I put our black helmets down on the floor and moved towards the children. The streets of the neighbourhood were a mix of mud and unfinished macadam works. It actually even looked like the works had only just started when it all ended, with two or three metres of paved road only. There were also six rusty electric engines, a few very big stones and some broken glass on the floor. One would actually wonder how kids could be left playing in such shameful and dangerous conditions.

The young man waved at the little boy, who recognised him right away, smiling happily. It seemed to me Federico knew everyone in town and everyone knew him too.

Federico asked the boy something, while giving him a big hug.

'*¡Hola Miguel! ¿Están tus padres alrededor ahora mismo?*'

'*Hola Federico,*' the child answered, jumping for joy, before adding some more Spanish. '*Si, está viendo en la casa.*'

Federico turned to me and translated that Miguel's father was in the house watching some television. Then he turned back to the boy and spoke again, apparently asking if we could speak with his father.

'*Entonces, ¿podemos hablar con tu padre?*'

'*Si, !siganme¡*'

The boy agreed and led the way to his parents' house. As with all the other houses in the street, the house looked quite simple and humble from the outside, with walls that were certainly old and frail, but very clean aside from a bit of graffiti here and there, with bars protecting the windows. When we went through the door, the temperature changed, it was definitely cooler. I noticed the air-conditioning system. The walls were blue everywhere. The volume of the television was so loud that we could hear it from the small corridor leading to the living room.

Miguel called out to his father who replied from the living room.

'Papi, ¡Federico y otro hombre quieren hablar contigo!'

'¡Dejalos entrar hijo!'

Miguel's father stood up from his sofa as we entered. Federico wrapped his arms strongly around our host to hug him. He was an old man with only a few white hairs left, a pair of small white glasses, and some particularly beautiful shiny teeth. He was wearing a brand new light-blue Nike jogging suit with brand new Nike trainers. He spoke warmly to Federico.

'Hola Federico, ¿Qué puedo hacer por ti? Y ¿quién es ese extranjero contigo?'

Federico introduced me to Ernesto Serez, who was looking at me with suspicion. While we were shaking hands, he explained that I was a journalist investigating the Swine Flu.

'El es un periodista investigando el virus de la Gripe porcina.'

Ernesto immediately pulled his hand back. As he was staring at me, he subtly took Federico away from the living room to have a serious chat with him. I could see that he wasn't really happy to see me.

'Federico, Yo pensé que lo había dejado claro... No mas periodistas, no mas expertos... ¡Por □evive!'

I couldn't understand their conversation because of the language barrier, but with the telly so loud, and the other children who came to play with Miguel, jumping around and screaming, it was hard to hear anyway. But deep down, I knew that Federico was going to plea for my cause. I had a really good feeling about that young man. Because of his behaviour, his self-confidence and his knowledge, I felt that I could actually trust him. It even came to my mind that he could be the real link to my understanding of the situation with the virus outbreak. He could actually be the key to the whole investigation.

I heard what they were saying, though of course, I didn't understand it.

'Espera, este hombre es diferente. ¡El está por encontrar la verdad! Y ¡el sabe acerca de los Aztlanes y el Proyecto de Aztlán!'

'Ok, entonces...'

Federico came back to explain that he had told Ernesto that I was seeking the truth. Ernesto had agreed to answer my questions. For the second time today, I was impressed by Federico's talent of persuasion. The old man turned off the television and asked all the children to leave the house.

55. Excerpt from *"The Aztlān Project"*.

CHAPTER 16.

"MORS TUA VITA MEA".

On 1st September 1534, Cardinal Campeggio and Pope Clement VII created the small council of the secretive dicastery called *In Pectore*. It consisted of five Cardinals nominated for life by the Pope, three co-opted Cardinals and the current Cardinal Secretary of State. Originally, the role of the nine Cardinals was to help the Pope choose the right Cardinal for Jaca. They were very well paid by the Vatican to help make that choice and to keep the secret alive.

In the seventeenth century, the council chose its motto: *"Mors Tua Vita Mea"*, which literally meant *"Your death, my life"*, or that *"where there is a battle for survival, your defeat is necessary for my survival..."*

Since its creation, *In Pectore* always knew everything of the existence of the organisation called *"The Aztlān Project"*. The Cardinals always managed to keep an eye on the Mexica. Century after century, they needed to keep them as far away from the hidden gold, and they always did.

Because of the early agreement between Pope Clement VII and King Charles V, the council had the responsibility of informing the current King of Spain of the name of the successors chosen for the Cardinalship of Jaca, who were the new soldiers of the Swiss Guard, and what was the secret password to open the special door of the hidden crypt of the cathedral.

The Cardinals always saw this duty as a real burden. As a rule, they were never involved with politics in Spain, but they did welcome the coups d'état and the establishment of two Spanish republics in 1873 and 1931, and most importantly, the authoritarian dictatorship of Francisco Franco in 1939. The mysterious dicastery indeed always believed that the end of the Spanish monarchy would also mean the end of the shared secret. For that reason, they always had a mole close to the King who knew everything the Cardinals needed to know. When in 1941, the death of King Alfonso XIII was announced, the nine Cardinals of the secret council exulted, for the death of the King of Spain meant that they and the Pope were the last to know about the secret treasure of Jaca. This meant the Vatican had full authority on it.

56. Patient zero.

11.28 a.m.

While Miguel's father was getting something for us to drink in the kitchen, Federico tried to clarify a few things for me. He said that the little boy was diagnosed with the virus in February, but other people had been ill for months. Poor people only, obviously. It spread really quickly within the community. Then, people started to die from what many in the region were already calling the *plague of the poor.*

'No one knew what that disease was,' he explained, looking through the window at the children playing in the street. 'Especially in a small community like ours where very few of us are actually educated. However, after a while, even the middle-class and the rich were catching the virus. The disease was spreading quicker and quicker, and more and more people were dying too.

'Eventually, the health authorities came to investigate and report everything back to the federal government. But when they visited the hospitals and hospices, they ordered the doctors and nurses to observe a complete black-out on the disease with regard to questions their patients and the media might ask about it. As the experts first thought that the respiratory disease was nothing more than pneumonia, they told them that no one should know anything about it until the federal government had made a decision. Then, the local authorities told the local media that they weren't allowed to report on the matter at all to avoid a wave of panic or paranoia among the population, unless they wanted the State's subsidies to stop. As for our community, when some of us asked the experts what the disease was, they told them it was a severe and unusual cold, and when asked if it could be influenza, they said it was impossible because influenza had been eradicated from Mexico!'

'Eradicated? That's quite an amazing statement!' I looked over at Ernesto, who was returning from the kitchen with some snack and drinks on a rolling tray.

'But at the beginning of March,' Federico continued, 'some people started to fall ill in the capital too, because, as you know, a lot of people from Santa Isabel Cholula actually work in Mexico City. So the *taboo* or *secret* of Santa Isabel Cholula totally blew apart. Besides, while it had certainly been child's play to mute the tiny media of Santa Isabel Cholula and its surroundings until then, it was obviously impossible to silence the big media engine of the capital.'

'Impossible to silence the media of the world altogether...'

'Exactly, and because viruses don't need a passport to cross a border, the virus then spread to other parts of the world, and you know the rest of story...'

'I unfortunately do. What about Miguel then?'

'After only a couple of days of illness, our little Miguel surprisingly recovered fully from the virus. That shocked absolutely everyone! Especially since nobody had yet recovered from the mysterious disease… When the local authorities heard the news, they sent health expert after health expert to check and double-check Miguel's health, and once they all acknowledged that the boy had miraculously survived the virus, the politicians got involved too.

'So the Governor of the state of Puebla, Fidel Alemán Morales, an old eccentric politician, visited this house with journalists, photographers, and TV and radio reporters. He was filmed for hours smiling at the cameras all the time, while taking the boy to school, helping him with his homework, and having lunch with his small family. During an interview for a foreign TV station, he even came up with the bizarre idea of erecting a statue made of concrete or bronze in the centre of Santa Isabel Cholula, in Miguel's honour, because he was the miraculous boy who survived the Swine Flu!'

My relationship with Ernesto warmed up a bit when he offered me a beer with a smile. It was a Sol, a very tasty beer. One of the best beers in Mexico according to what I had read in a guide.

I wanted to ask Federico a question.

'Federico, I must say that when we entered the house earlier, I felt a real shock at the display of luxurious decorations here and there, the use of modern technology in this room, and the branded clothes Miguel's father is wearing, compared to the absolute abysmal poverty of the neighbourhood. Was that all due to the Governor's generosity?'

'Yes, it was,' the young man confirmed, giving me a small ceramic bowl with peanuts and cashew nuts. 'The flat screen TV, the brand new kitchen appliances, the washing machine, the air-conditioning, the clothes, and the shoes… all this comes from the Governor's *goodness*. It was obviously a way for him to display his kind-heartedness to the population of Puebla, and furthermore to the whole of Mexico! Let's not forget that there will be an election in 2010 to choose our new Governor, and as

Governor Morales started his campaign in January this year, you can only imagine the boost the sensational recovery of a poor four-year-old boy, who he would have visited and played with, and more importantly, whose family would get financial support from his government, can give to his campaign!'

I started having serious doubts about my *Aztlān theory*. I just couldn't see where the Aztlāns could fit in the virus story anymore. We had a small community of poor people living in a small town in the middle of nowhere. Then we had a multinational company polluting the community with the wastes from its big pig farm. We also had local and federal authorities taking wrong decisions because they didn't take the community's health warnings about the farm seriously. And to finish, we had a virus that spread in Mexico, and in the rest of the world, after both the farm and the authorities failed to protect the people of Santa Isabel Cholula. The Swine Flu story sounded more and more to me like the ordinary case of a multimillion-dollar company denying its polluting actions, combined with some slow and corrupted politicians committing error after error because of their ignorance of the Swine Flu problem, and less like a conspiracy.

57. Excerpt from *"The Aztlān Project"*.

CHAPTER 17.

THE VATICAN BANK.

In 1942, under the strong recommendation of the nine Cardinals of the secretive *In Pectore*, Pope Pius XII founded The *Istituto per le Opere di Religione* – commonly known as the *"Vatican Bank"* – whose aim was *"to provide for the safekeeping and administration of movable and immovable property transferred or entrusted to it by physical or juridical persons and intended for works of religion or charity"*. It was run by a bank director who had to report directly to the nine Cardinals, and ultimately to the Pope.

However, the real reason behind the creation of the bank was to discreetly increase the investments of the Vatican around the globe, and even more discreetly make the Cardinals' earnings grow. Even though the Vatican had always paid their salaries and all their expenditures, the nine Cardinals suddenly felt that they deserved significantly more for keeping such an important and critical secret. As secrets don't pay…

Without the Spanish monarchy to worry about any longer, the secret council also decided that it was about time they got seriously involved with the running of the world. Thus, another aim of the Vatican Bank was to fund political parties, trade unions, and guerrillas in communist countries to free them from the big red threat, even if it was at the price of immoral associations or friendships, or worse, corruption.

Unfortunately for the Cardinals, everything started going wrong when Pope John Paul I became pontiff in 1978. As he knew about the allegations of wrongdoing at the bank, he mandated his Cardinal Secretary of State to investigate the matter thoroughly, vowing that he would dismiss senior Vatican officials if necessary. That very Cardinal was one of the nine Cardinals of *In Pectore*. Pope John Paul I died of a heart attack after only 33 days in office, according to original press reports of his death. The Vatican opposed any idea of a papal autopsy as being prohibited under Vatican law. As to the enquiry on the Vatican Bank, it was simply cancelled by his successor, John Paul II.

But in 1982, the bank was involved in a major political and financial scandal, when Banco Ambrosiano (of which it was the major shareholder) collapsed and lost $3.5 billion. Furthermore, the head of the bank at the time, Father Marcinkus, failed to be brought to justice as the Italian courts ruled that because he was a high-ranking prelate of the Vatican, he had diplomatic immunity from Italian prosecution. He retired in Sun City, Arizona, where he died in 2006. Later, the Vatican bank paid $241 million to its creditors.

In September 1983, the nine Cardinals decided on an important transaction they wanted the bank to deal with: the selling of almost half of the treasure of Jaca to the Far East. In total, 6,800 gold bars were sold to Hong Kong's largest independent local bank, worth more than $36 million.

Reserves of gold had grown in importance in the country since intensified political talk over Hong Kong's handover of sovereignty back to China from the United Kingdom had resulted in an uncertain fluctuation in the domestic currency.

58. DNA.

11.43 a.m.

I still wanted to check on one last thing I had a few doubts on: my genetically targeted virus theory.

I asked Federico if Ernesto would allow his son's DNA to be analysed by a friend of mine who worked in a laboratory in London. As I didn't really want to get into the details of my theory, especially the Aztlān part because Federico had told me that he didn't know anything about them when we were at the café, I tried to sum it up for them. The young man was translating everything back to Ernesto.

'In fact, I would like to test Miguel's DNA to know whether the virus is actually targeting some people and not others; targeting the people of Santa Isabel Cholula in particular. Because as far as I can see, your town was the location the most hit by the virus by far. I'll send the DNA sample to my good friend in London who will analyse it with some other samples of people who fell ill or who died of the virus in Europe, and I'll get the results quickly after.'

Federico turned to Ernesto and started explaining what I wanted to do.

'Ernesto, Sergio me dijo esta mañana que un hombre vendría a ver a Miguel pronto.'

While the young man was talking, Ernesto was looking at me in what I would describe as a funny way. Federico was still speaking.

'El dijo que el hombre ha sido muy engañado por gente mala y que el vendría a Santa Isabel Cholula con el extraño pensamiento que los Aztlanes han creado el virus para matar a los descendientes de los Tlaxcalanes.'

I was now getting Ernesto's upset look again. I was wondering whether Federico was actually translating what I had just said or if something else was going on... I was quite sure I had heard Federico saying *Aztlān* somewhere in a sentence.

'Y el dijo que si el hombre iba a pedir la prueba del ADN de Miguel nosotros deberíamos de aceptarlo, asi que el entiende que los Aztlanes no son los chicos malos.'

I quickly interrupted Federico as I thought he might have been trying to push Ernesto not to let me do the test.

'Federico, please, tell him that it is a very simple and harmless test,' I told him with my pitiful eyes directed on Miguel's father. 'I will only need a couple of hairs from Miguel's head. That's it. It really is nothing. Believe me, Ernesto!'

'Ernesto, ese hombre, el periodista, es el que la organización ha escogido para finalmente descubrir donde esta el tesoro perdido! ¡Nosotros no podemos dejarlo caer ahora después de todo lo que ha hecho por nosotros y por nuestra gente! Aztlán debe gracias a nosotros, gracias a ti!'

I was now absolutely certain that I had heard Federico say *Aztlān* at least twice during his conversation. Ernesto suddenly stood up and took three steps in my direction. When he stopped in front of me, my heart stopped too. I thought that whatever Federico had just told him was going to land me in big trouble.

Then he surprisingly shook hands with me with a very big smile on his face. He was even nodding his head as I thanked him. That was something I wasn't expecting from him.

Very suddenly, we felt a light tremor in the house. Everything started trembling gently. Then some items and frames fell on the floor. I even thought that the window behind me was going to shake into pieces by the noise it was making hitting its own frame. But Federico told me not to worry, to stay calm, and seated while the light earthquake hit us. He explained that this wasn't anything major in any way and that the epicentre was certainly quite far from the town.

Federico was right. When it stopped after a minute or two, we all stood up to tidy up. As I stood up, I awkwardly knocked over my beer on the yellow carpet with my left knee. Then, while I was cleaning my mess, the little blue book fell out of my pocket and onto the floor. When I realised they could see the title of the book on its velvet-like cover, I mechanically turned to the two men standing in front of me, whose smiles had turned into frowns. They were now staring at me with inevitable suspicion.

59. Breaking News.

Magnus Press Agency, UK.

The US Geological Survey, which monitors earthquake activity worldwide, said on Monday that Mexico had been hit by a 5.8 magnitude earthquake, just 19 miles south-southeast of Tixtla, about 150 miles south of the capital, Mexico City. According to media reports, most buildings in the capital shook during the quake.

60. Excerpt from *"The Aztlān Project"*.

CHAPTER 18.

THE THIEVES OF SOUTH LONDON.

On 16th November 1983, the gold for Hong Kong was discreetly transferred by some trusted militaries of the Swiss Guard, from Jaca to Toulouse, then to Nantes, and then on to London. There, it was locked in a gigantic safe, deep inside a secure *Brinks Mat* building surrounded by guards, at Heathrow Airport.

Just ten days later, on 26th November, six men broke into the warehouse, with the help of an inside man. In no time, the gang disabled the guards and tied them up. Then to force them to reveal the combination to the safe, they poured petrol over them and threatened them with lighted matches until they gave in. When the safe was finally opened, they found three tonnes of gold and a lot of cut and uncut diamonds, exactly what they were after. Two hours later, the gang finally made their getaway.

The brains of the gang, Mickey McAvoy and Brian Robinson, were both already quite well-known to the police. So to have any chance of getting away with this robbery, the robbers had to arrange for the booty to be discreetly laundered and then transferred into their pockets. But the two South London men seriously lacked subtlety and discretion. Before the robbery, they were living in modest council houses in London, then a few weeks later, they moved to a very large house in Kent, paid for in cash. Also, McAvoy had bought two Rottweiler dogs to protect his mansion. He named them *"Brinks"* and *"Mat"*.

Scotland Yard quickly discovered how the robbery was conceived and who was behind it. After being arrested and tried at the Old Bailey in London, Robinson and McAvoy were each sentenced to 25 years imprisonment for armed robbery, while the other four robbers were never convicted.

Some of the gold was eventually recovered, but most of the three tonnes stolen by the gang went missing, and this is why the case remains open today. Each one-kilo ingot had been refined in Spain at the *Sociedad Española de Metales Preciosos*, and had both the seal of the Spanish company and a serial number engraved on it.

The truth behind the gold robbery was that it had actually been planned and financed by a wealthy individual who knew everything about the secret of Jaca, the Vatican, and the Aztlān Project. That robbery was his first attempt to make the Vatican know that he was on a mission…

As for the Hong Kong bank, they never received their gold and they legitimately asked the Vatican Bank for an outrageous but righteous amount of compensation afterwards. After the unfortunate incident, in August 1985, the nine current Cardinals of the secretive *In Pectore* decided to get their act together and leave the administration of the bank to some real professionals. The wise men also pledged that their council should never get involved in money or politics again, as this would undoubtedly lead to their exposure and their downfall.

61. A typical family meal.

12.11 p.m.

The men were now talking discreetly to each other, confident that I couldn't understand them.

'¿Qué es este libro?' asked Ernesto. *'Esta escrito en Inglés, pero seguramente puedo leer Aztlán en el.'*

'No lo se, Ernesto,' Federico replied. *'Solo hay que pretender que nosotros no vimos nada.'*

Then they turned back to me with surprising smiles upon their faces.

'Please… don't worry about the carpet, Señor Duprés!' Federico told me, as he was discreetly pointing at the kitchen with his thumb for Miguel's father to go.

'We'll clean that in a minute,' he added. 'Ernesto just asked me if you would like to stay with us for lunch. By the smell in the kitchen, I think his wife has prepared some Tamale. Have you ever eaten Tamale?'

I suspected that something was going on, but because of the language barrier, I couldn't really be sure. I immediately put the book back in my jeans' pocket and accepted the invitation.

I met Ernesto's wife, Aloisa, in the kitchen. She was a large, smiling forty-year-old lady, who Federico said cooked like a chef. She would stand for hours in the kitchen just to prepare the family meal.

She greeted me rapidly and instantly got me sitting at the dining table, with a plate of Tamale in front of me. Tamale was a dish of starchy dough, corn-based, steamed in plantain leaves. It was rather square, quite firm, and had a savoury pork filling. Tamale was considered one of the most beloved traditional foods in Mexico.

The dining room quickly filled up as several children showed up from nowhere to eat some of the chips Aloisa had placed in three baskets at the centre of the table.

All of a sudden, the mother shouted something in Spanish. Everybody immediately stopped talking. The six children were asked to go to the living room, where she took their food. Some of them sat on the two sofas, others on the floor in front of the television, which was now showing cartoons. Then Aloisa, back in the dining room, served us the barbecued shrimps, rice, and black beans with a very hot Cholula sauce that she had been preparing since eight o'clock in the morning. That was an outstanding, yet simple meal.

It was a great time for me to take a rest from all that had been happening for the last few hours. After lunch, Ernesto gave me a small transparent plastic bag with some hair he had cut from Miguel's head. I left shortly afterwards with Federico.

Before heading back to my hotel room in Tlaxcala by taxi, I wanted to have a word with the people at the big farm outside the town. Federico agreed to take me there.

"He that communicates his secret to another makes himself that other's slave."
– Baltasar Gracián (1601-1658)

CHAPTER 6. THE CODEX

Codex [noun] – a manuscript, or a volume of manuscripts of ancient holy writing.

(Excerpt from the Storyteller Dictionary)

62. Excerpt from *"The Aztlān Project"*.

CHAPTER 19.

THE HOUSE OF BORGIA: AN INFAMOUS DYNASTY.

The House of Borja (*Borja* became *Borgia* in Italian) was a Spanish-Italian noble, influential, and prominent family during the Renaissance period that spread over the 14th through to the 17th century. Its family members are notorious for their endless practice of nepotism: a practice that the Catholic Church had been observing since the Middle Age, where some popes and bishops were giving their nephews or other relatives positions of preference within the church in order to continue a dynasty. They were also noted for their involvement with various highly significant crimes in Europe, mostly including corruption, but also adultery, theft, simony, bribery, incest, rape and murder. Murder by poison in particular.

63. At the farm…

1.43 p.m.

As we arrived at the farm, I noticed the heavily electrified gate, which was secured by a CCTV system of about twenty cameras and six or seven guards in a light brown and black uniform. Wearing sunglasses, having small moustaches, smoking cigarettes, and playing with their electric prods seemed to be the sole requirements to work for Granja Dodgson's security. They were all seated in the shadow of a huge sign in Spanish and in English that said: *"Do not trespass. Private property. You have been warned!"*

What exactly were they protecting there? A prison, a bank, some jewellery? What precious gems or treasure were they watching over? Pigs?

From a distance, I could see a tractor in the fields as well as hundreds of large silver buildings. There was no noise coming from the farm, just the wind rocking the graceful green grass, in front of the gate. The wind was also blowing that strong smell of swine that I had experienced when I arrived by taxi earlier.

Another thing that I noticed was that the road from the town to the farm was dusty and unfinished, while the road from the farm to the cities around was perfectly macadamised and clean.

Federico stopped his motorbike on the opposite side of the road. We crossed the lane to go and speak to the gang of security guards, who were now staring at us, suspiciously. As we had crossed half the road, one of them shouted something at us. Federico stopped me suddenly.

Then the two men exchanged some strong words, Federico later told me. He asked for someone from the farm to come and speak to me, but the guard refused, telling him to go away while we could. When Federico stepped forward, they all stood up and took their electric prods in hand. They looked pretty angry and not at all pleased to see us still standing in the middle of the road despite their warning.

There was no traffic on that road, so we didn't need to worry about getting run over by a car. But at that moment, I indeed thought that I was going to get beaten up and crucified by the gang.

They all switched on their electric prods before moving towards us. Their sadistic manners were getting me worried. Federico and I stepped back when all of a sudden, the telephone rang in the security booth by the entrance of the farm. They all froze and one of the guards attended the call. After talking to someone for less than a minute, the guard shouted something to his colleagues.

Federico told me they were going to let us in. At first, they were as surprised as we were, but then their ugly faces changed into smiles and their roughness became kindness. There was such a contrast that I wondered if it was actually one of their tricks to assault us afterwards.

The guards opened the gateway in front of us, but I kept looking at them as we walked through the gate. Trust no one. As I was watching the large iron door closing behind us, I noticed that a black car with tinted windows had parked outside the farm, close to Federico's motorbike.

Three men dressed in black suits got out of the SUV. All three men were bald.

64. Excerpt from *"The Aztlān Project"*.

CHAPTER 20.

THE HOUSE OF BORGIA.

1. ALFONSO.

Alfonso de Borja y Cavanilles was born in 1378, in the neighbourhood of Valencia, which was then the Kingdom of Valencia under the Crown of Aragon, today's Spain. A university law professor, he quickly became a lawyer and a diplomat in the service of King Alfonso V of Aragon. After a successful mission to end the Western Schism, a split within the Roman Catholic Church that nearly lasted 70 years, he was awarded the bishopric of Valencia before becoming the King's Vice-Chancellor and Royal adviser.

In 1444, Pope Eugenio IV named him Cardinal, before he finally rose to the papal chair, in 1455, as Pope *Callixtus III*. Some of his decisions were very controversial. For example, his papal bull *"Inter Caetera"* to Portugal authorised the Portuguese to reduce all infidels to servitude, giving tacit consent that the enslavement of Africans wasn't contradictory to the word of God, nor to the teaching of the Church.

Practicing nepotism since when he was a Cardinal, Pope Callixtus III also made his nephew, Rodrigo Borgia, Cardinal. Callixtus III was the first member of the House of Borgia to hold such an important position. His papacy lasted three years, until he died in 1458.

2. RODRIGO.

Roderic Llançol, also known as Rodrigo Borgia, was born in 1431, in the Kingdom of Valencia. He studied law and became successively Bishop, Cardinal, and Vice-Chancellor of the Church, after his uncle's election as Pope. He served in the Roman Curia for five papacies and gained influence and wealth.

When Pope Innocent VIII died in 1492, he was among the only three candidates for the Papacy. Thanks to his great wealth, he bought the largest number of votes and became Pope, assuming the name of *Alexander VI*. At the time, Giovanni di Lorenzo de Medici, who later became Pope Leo X, said of Alexander VI: *"Now, we are in the power of a wolf, the most rapacious perhaps that this world has ever seen. And if we do not flee, he will inevitably devour us all."*

A series of confiscations was set up by the Pope, because he needed funds to carry out his policies. Anyone known to be rich, including cardinals, noblemen, or any official, was accused of some offence, jailed or murdered, and then their properties were confiscated. Any opposition to Borgia was punished with death. A radical monk, Girolamo Savonarola, appealed for a general council to confront the papal abuses and corruption, but Alexander VI excommunicated him, bullied the Florentine government, and the monk was then condemned to death.

Pope Alexander VI was the first pope to openly acknowledge that he had had four children by his long-time mistress Vannozza dei Cattani, countess of the House of Candia. He died aged 72, poisoned by his own son, Cesare Borgia, at a Cardinal Adriano de Fornetto's dinner, in 1503.

3. FRANCESCO.

Francesco Borgia de Candia y Aragon was born in 1510, in the Kingdom of Valencia. Francesco was the great-grandson of Pope Alexander VI. The child wanted to become a monk, but his family sent him to the court of the Holy Roman Emperor Charles V. There, he distinguished himself, accompanying the Emperor on several campaigns. In 1539, he was made Viceroy of Catalonia, but when his father died, he retired to his native land and led a life devoted entirely to Jesus Christ and the Catholic Church, along with his wife and eight children,.

When his wife died in 1546, Francesco entered the newly formed *Society of Jesus*. He renounced his titles in favour of his eldest son, Carlos, and became a Jesuit priest. In 1565, he became Father General of the *Society of Jesus*.

Francesco Borgia (also known as *Francis*) died in 1572, in Rome. He was beatified in Madrid in 1624, by Pope Gregory XV and canonized in 1670, by Pope Clement X.

4. STEFANO.

Stefano Borgia was born in 1731, in the small city of Velletri, near Rome. A direct descendent of Francesco Borgia, his early education was controlled by his uncle Alessandro Borgia, Archbishop of Fermo. Stefano had a strong taste for historical research and for relics of ancient civilisations. Following his father's example, throughout his life, he gathered antiquities in a museum that he founded in Velletri.

Pope Benedict XIV appointed Stefano Governor of Benevento, before making him Secretary of the *Propagation of the Faith* at the Vatican; an office that he took advantage of to acquire even more antiquities with the help of the church's missionaries. Then in 1789, he was made a Cardinal and joined the Vatican's *In Pectore*.

But in 1804, while travelling in France, Stefano was suddenly taken ill and died. After his death, his collection of manuscripts was split between two locations: the *"non-Biblical"* manuscripts were taken to the *Biblioteca Borbonica* in Naples (now the *Biblioteca nazionale Vittorio Emanuele III*) and the *"Biblical"* manuscripts, collections of coins, and monuments were taken to the *Roman Curia*'s offices, at the Vatican. If during the twentieth century most manuscripts were transferred from the *Roman Curia* to the *Vatican Library*, one document has been missing from the inventories of Stefano's properties, before being replaced by a fake at the *Vatican Library*: a mysterious Mexica *Codex*.

65. Double-talk.

2.08 p.m.

We were approaching the only office building of the farm when three women dressed in medical white coats came to greet us. All three women were tall brunettes. One of them was wearing glasses.

They introduced themselves to Federico as being two senior nutritionists and the farm's spokeswoman.

Federico explained in Spanish who I was and why I had asked to meet them. They immediately switched to English and turned to me.

'Welcome to Granja Dodgson, Señor Duprés!' the spokeswoman announced with a wide smile on her face. 'My name is Victoria, this is Manuela and this is Teresa. Would you like to visit our facilities?'

'Well… may I have a moment with you first to ask you a few questions about the farm?' I asked.

'Of course,' she answered simply. 'Please follow me to our office.'

We then entered the building where the doors and walls were adorned with Spanish signs warning *"No entry!"*

I had a last look at the men in black outside only to notice that they had mysteriously gone. I wondered what was going on.

A fat old lady was cleaning the floor in the corridor. As we walked past her, she smiled at me. We entered a room where every desk was very tidy and equipped with a brand new laptop, a telephone, and a printer-fax machine. There were walls everywhere and only one small window. About twenty people were working there. I immediately recognised the lay-out of the room and concluded that it was the farm's press office. There was some kind of music in the quasi-silent background.

We entered another room with a large bay window giving a view onto the farm's fields. Only one desk there. The sun was shining and the temperature outside was almost unbearable at 38° or 40° Celsius.

We all sat there on very comfortable chairs around a large square table. An assistant brought us some coffee and biscuits and served everyone. Then she left and, as she closed the door, Victoria started the conversation.

'Señor Duprés, you said that you have some questions for us?'

'Oh, just a few really...' I answered, sipping my coffee before asking my first question.

'I'm really interested in knowing what it is that you produce in this farm.'

'Our mother company, Virginia Foods, is the largest pork producer in Mexico and the United States,' Victoria explained. 'Our farm is exclusively dedicated to selling swine that has not yet been slaughtered. Then the pigs are sent to slaughterhouses. Everything we produce on this farm is sold on the Mexican market, 60% of which is traded in the capital and the state of Mexico.'

'As any other farms in the world, your farm must be producing a lot of chemical and non-chemical wastes, right?' She nodded her head and I continued. 'Would you then consider it possible that this farm is somehow polluting the town of Santa Isabel Cholula?'

The three women looked at each other for a couple of seconds, before Teresa, one of the senior nutritionists, answered. 'I can frankly tell you, with a certain pride, that our farm has won an award last year – the *"America Green Evaluation Award"* to be precise – for our long-term commitment to environmental protection.'

Then Victoria continued.

'What we try to accomplish here is coexistence, respect, and conservation between our activity and the surrounding ecosystem. We do our best to protect the communities around our facilities and we have also developed a reforestation program, which benefits the environment and the people involved. We have won this award for the fourth consecutive year!'

That sounded just like a press release taken from a standard press kit.

'May I ask you who organises these awards?' I asked, really intrigued.

'Of course, it is a well-known US company called *Anzules Group*,' the spokeswoman replied.

66. Excerpt from *"The Aztlān Project"*.

CHAPTER 21.

THE MISSING CODICES.

The missing Codex was brought to Europe by Hernán Cortés in 1528, when King Charles V, fearing that he was becoming too powerful in the New World, forced him to return to Spain. To show his respect and his admiration to his King, Cortés offered him some golden pieces of jewellery as well as two ancient Mesoamerican manuscripts. All items had been stolen from the defeated Mexica Emperor, Moctezuma II.

Cortés' wife, a native from the New World, had told him that one of the manuscripts had significant importance for the Mexicas. It was called *Codex Teōtīhuacān* (*Teōtīhuacān* is Nahuatl for *"the birthplace of the gods"*) and, according to the most learned Mexica scholars, it had always been regarded as the rulers of Tenochtitlán *Tlatoanis'* most valuable possession.

The 76-page Codex that was to be read from right to left was made of animal skins folded into 39 sheets, with all but the end sheets painted on both sides. It was said to have been written by the *Toltecs*, the Mexicas' ancestors, around the tenth or the twelfth century. It was believed to contain mysterious rituals, divinatory sacred texts, and enigmatic scriptures.

The understanding of the meaning of the Codex has always been the number one objective of the Spaniards since its discovery, but because of the obvious lack of any comparable document, it led to a variety of interpretations. When King Charles V received the Codex, he asked his closest adviser, Francesco Borgia, to enrol the cleverest scholars of the Kingdom to find out what the mysterious meaning of the Codex was. But they all failed.

Charles V, who didn't want to waste time, energy, and money on what he eventually thought was a useless matter, gave the two codices to Francesco. He decided to keep the manuscripts among his other properties until he entered the *Society of Jesus* to become a Jesuit priest, at which time, he gave everything to his eldest son, Carlos.

Passed from one generation to another, the Codex Borgia and the mysterious Codex, secretly safeguarded by the Borgias, ended up in the hands of Cardinal Stefano Borgia, who was himself absolutely passionate about relics of ancient civilisations and created a museum of antiquities.

Because he never told them anything about it, when the other Cardinals of *In Pectore* overheard a conversation where Stefano Borgia mentioned the existence of the precious and mysterious manuscript, they simply ordered his assassination so they could take over the Codex.

After his death, the German naturalist and explorer Alexander von Humboldt discovered the two codices among the effects of the Cardinal. One was the Codex Borgia and the other one was a fake that the other Cardinals, who had split Stefano Borgia's properties and transferred most manuscripts to the *Vatican Library*, had created.

As for the mysterious Codex, since then it has been secretly kept in a hidden office of the *Roman Curia* where the Vatican's experts have been working on its impenetrable esoteric meaning for decades, without success.

*"All that is necessary for the triumph of evil
is for good men to do nothing."*
– Edmund Burke (1729-1797)

CHAPTER 7. INFLUENCE

Influence [noun] – the power resulting from the ability of a person to affect others, or to use personal connections in order to manipulate people.

(Excerpt from the Storyteller Dictionary)

67. Anzules Group.

2.31 p.m.

'Anzules Group, you said...' I repeated, while quickly browsing my iPhone's Internet. 'You see, I just typed the words *"Anzules Group"* on the Internet and within a couple of seconds, I got hundreds of pages with information about that company. Isn't it fabulous?'

Everybody smiled. I wasn't smiling. I quickly explained my reaction to my audience... I had just discovered that, if indeed Anzules Group was organising an award ceremony in Mexico City to award the greenest companies in the country, there was some confusion in the media about the fairness of the awards. Confusion due to the fact that the farm belonged to the US company *Virginia Foods*, which itself was bought ten years earlier by a Guatemalan company called *Grupo Borgia*. And I knew that the Anzules Group was the mother company of Grupo Borgia...

'Well… that is interesting…' stammered the farm's spokeswoman, looking rather embarrassed. 'I would need to double-check that information, obviously…'

'Obviously,' I answered ironically.

'Any more questions, maybe?' she asked, trying to change the subject of our conversation.

I didn't hesitate and threw in my coup de grace.

'How could you prove to me that the farm isn't the source of the Swine Flu virus?'

I noticed that Federico was particularly enjoying this time with me in the press office.

'The Mexican authorities sent experts to Santa Isabel Cholula when the virus started to spread a few weeks ago,' Teresa answered. 'These scientists then visited the farm in recent weeks and tested all our pigs. They have found no evidence that any one of them was the source of the virus. Besides, we ourselves operate a very rigorous control on our pigs every week. Our policy regarding pigs infected by any kind of disease is extremely strict. Any occurrence of a disease in any of our lots would immediately stop our production. Every single pig of the suspected lot would be destroyed by cremation, and a thorough check of all the other lots would take place before any decision to restart the production is taken.'

'Such a situation did not occur in the past weeks,' Manuela concluded, the quietest of the three women. 'That is our ultimate proof that the Swine Flu virus didn't originate on our farm. And that certainly also closes our conversation now…'

She stood up and everybody else stood up too. It was hard to believe that that woman was only a senior nutritionist at the farm. She seemed to have more influence on everybody than they wanted to let us know. I still had one or two questions to ask, but it really didn't seem to be the right moment. As we were leaving the room with the other two women following our steps, Manuela quickly left. The only thing that came to my mind at that moment was that she wasn't really from the farm; she was only there with us to listen to my questions and see if I knew anything that they were hiding.

The two women escorted us to the gate where we met our friends with their electric prods again. The guys didn't look too pleased to see us go. They would have certainly preferred it if we could have provided them with a chance to actually use their weapons on us. As for my other friends, the bald men in black, they had left no traces of their passing in the area. It all looked like it had been a figment of my imagination.

We eventually climbed on Federico's motorbike and set off for the little town. From there, I was to take a taxi back to Tlaxcala.

68. Excerpt from *"The Aztlān Project"*.

CHAPTER 22 – FINAL CHAPTER.

A MAN ON A MISSION.

In 1975, a boy called Rodrigo Stefano Borgia Anzules was born in Guatemala City. The boy's father was Fernando Enrique Anzules from Guatemala, and his mother was Estela Marisa Borgia from Mexico. Rodrigo was a descendent of the House of Borgia through Cardinal Stefano Borgia's branch.

Rodrigo started selling strawberry jam, door-to-door, at the age of nine. He collected and bottled the jam from an old neighbour and used labels that he printed in his father's office in Guatemala's Central Bank. Early in life, he also acquired a great passion for reading, especially history books, and for collecting all sorts of antiquities from the Spanish Conquest of Mexico.

At 16, he went to study at *The American School of Guatemala*, one of the most expensive private schools in Central America. After that, he crossed the Atlantic Ocean and obtained a MBA at the London Business

School before being employed at Deloitte as an auditor for a year. At that time, he came to realise that the only thing he wanted to be was an entrepreneur.

In 1996, Rodrigo Anzules returned to Guatemala where he founded *Grupo Anzules*, a company selling appliances, electronics, and furniture all over the country. Through providing credit sales, he rapidly developed a vast consumer market. After this first success, Anzules decided to buy ten companies that were on the verge of bankruptcy. He made them profitable and changed his focus to expand into new fields.

In 2000, the company moved to the US market. The headquarters subsequently moved to New York and the company's name changed to *Anzules Group and* it became a US company.

At the same time, in Guatemala, Anzules created a new company called *Grupo Borgia* to sell his products in stores all over the country, while Anzules Group was to become its mother company. In 2002, the Finance Ministry granted Grupo Borgia a banking license so it could operate simultaneously in 900 branch offices located in its stores. Banco Borgia was thus born. Grupo Borgia instantly became Guatemala's biggest consumer-finance company.

In 2002, the first *America Green Evaluation Awards* were presented by Anzules Group to companies supporting and implementing new environmental rules and ideas at work. Between 2005 and 2009, a swine farm in Mexico called *Granja Dodgson* consistently received the award, even though its mother company belonged to Grupo Borgia.

In 2003, Rodrigo Anzules received a civil society medal from the United Nations for the *"Anzules Walk to Beat Breast Cancer"*, an event organised in twenty-nine cities in the United States and thirty-two other cities in the world by his non-profit organisation, Fundación Borgia.

During the noughties, Anzules Group kept expanding in Guatemala, in Mexico, as well as in the US in various businesses, creating TV and radio networks (*TV Borgia, Radio Borgia,* and *Borgia America*), newspapers (Diario de Borgia, La voz de Borgia, and Borgia News International), banks and insurance companies (*Seguro Borgia* and *Borgia Bank America*), telecommunication companies (*Borgia Telecom,*

BorgiaTfoni, and *Borgia Telecom International*) and finally, Internet providers (*BorgiaNet* and *Borgia On Line*).

In 2008, Anzules even received the *"Good Neighbour Award"* from the US Guatemalan Commerce Chamber.

Today, Rodrigo Stefano Borgia Anzules is one of Forbes *World's Richest People.* He serves as President and CEO of Anzules Group and Grupo Borgia, two holdings with interests placed in retail stores, media, finances, real estate, telecommunications, new technologies, and more recently, the pharmaceutical industry. Anzules is Latin America's leading entrepreneur. He is very influential politically since he counts many of his friends amongst the two major political parties in Guatemala and Mexico, and he is regularly advising the two governments on economic, media, and foreign policies.

Anzules' only known dark side, so far, has been his involvement in a series of political and financial scandals, including a famous corruption case when he was trying to obtain his banking license from the Mexican Finance Ministry. He is also rumoured to have created and trained a secret militia of about five or six hundred men, whose sole task is to do his dirty work for him. An example of that was when he and a gang of about fifty bald men were accused of taking over the facilities of a factory that he had just bought in 2001, in Ciudad Juárez, with violence. Neither of these two cases, nor any other since, ever incriminated Anzules directly.

Let's not forget that this is the man who once said in an interview live on *CNN en Español*, when talking about the many law suits against him that were being examined by some of the top judges in Mexico: *"I don't care about these judges and I don't care about their justice. I know that they will never find me guilty, because I believe that no one is more above justice than I am, not even God!"*

69. The message.

6.13 p.m.

Back to my hotel in Tlaxcala, I had a lie-down on my bed for a good half an hour. After going to the laundry to clean my dirty smelly clothes, I took a well-deserved shower.

After my shower, I left the shower cubicle and grabbed a towel hanging at the door of the bathroom. The room was so steamy that I couldn't see my face on the mirror. However, I could read some words there. Someone had written something on my mirror that would only appear when the room was steamed up.

Banorte Sucursal Merced – Mexico

072-133-00001024052

What was that all about? I stormed out of the bathroom without a towel, looking for a pen and a piece of paper somewhere in my trousers so I could write the message down before it disappeared.

'I can wait outside, if you need time to get ready,' a feminine voice announced right behind me.

I turned around and saw *DoctorVanity1918* sitting on my bed and staring at me stood there naked, pen in one hand, some paper in the other hand.

I stormed back in the bathroom, put the towel around my hips, and while writing the message, took the time to answer with the cap of my pen in the mouth.

'Sorry for the outfit, I just didn't think anyone would be waiting for me in my room without having been invited, that's all!'

'I didn't know I needed an invitation!'

'You don't,' I replied, trying to correct my words. 'It's just that I really didn't expect anyone in my room this evening. Especially not you!'

'Tlaxcala is a very nice city. And as a matter of fact, I was born here…'

'Really?' I asked, trying to reach around the bathroom door to get my clothes from the chair.

'Really. Why are so surprised?'

'I think that you mentioned the Mexicas and the Tlaxcalans were enemies before the Spanish Conquest of Mexico in your little blue book. And as you had strong words to describe the Tlaxcalans as losers because they had chosen to ally themselves with the Spaniards, I thought that Tlaxcala was certainly the last place on Earth where you would ever try to find me!'

'I see that you know who wrote the little blue book,' she replied, sounding like she was smiling. 'What else do you know?'

Through the steamy mirror, I could at last see my face. During the last few weeks, I had become quite tanned due to a lot of time spent in the sun, and with my mid-length hair and my small goatee, I now looked very much like Robert Downey Jr.

I eventually came out of the bathroom, dressed in my usual jeans and white t-shirt. She was still there, sitting on my bed in a posh pastel skirt, a white blouse, and pastel shoes, her small black Louis Vuitton bag on her side. With her long hair and her shiny eyes, the young woman looked quite elegant, but quite charming too. As at our first meeting, she smelled of vanilla.

I had just met her twice until now, but I still didn't know what her name was, whereas she knew my name. Something else I wasn't sure about was whether she knew about the message on the mirror, so I put the paper in my pocket and thoroughly erased the message from the mirror.

'Would you like to have dinner with me?' I asked, cheekily. 'I'll tell you what I know over a nice bottle of wine if you want.'

'I am afraid I cannot stay for dinner. I cannot be seen with you otherwise they will kill us both!'

'Who are *they*?'

'Jean-Baptiste, did you read Chapter 22, the final chapter of the book?'

'The one about the entrepreneur from Guatemala? Yes, I did. Why? Is he also involved in the Swine Flu story?'

'Let me put it in a clear way for you to understand: Anzules is the only person involved in the story! Very badly involved!'

I couldn't believe what I had just heard… How could that man be the only person involved in the story? I needed some explanations.

'Wait a second, in your book, you first told me everything about the Mexicas and the Spanish Conquest. Then you talked about the Aztlān organisation and their people who want to avenge their ancestors. Suddenly you bring in a secret organisation within the Vatican, before talking about a family dynasty and a Codex. You end the book introducing me to a man who is one of the richest men in the world, and who you now suggest is in fact the villain behind it all. I'm afraid I can't quite understand why you had to tell me all these things about the Mexicas and the Vatican then?'

'That's something you will soon understand. I know it might still be very unclear to you right now, but believe me; it will all make sense in the end…'

The woman looked at her watch anxiously and announced that she had to leave.

'We will meet again in Mexico,' she concluded, before leaving the room like the wind.

As she left, I couldn't stop thinking about what she had just said. It was really confusing. Anzules was involved? Why? Had I missed something in the book? Did I somehow miss the link between Anzules and the virus? Did I need to read the book again?

Besides, I was still wondering who had left the message on the mirror. Certainly not her, she would have definitely told me something about it. Who then? The Aztlāns? The men in black? Anybody else?

I browsed the internet on my iPhone to check what *"Banorte Sucursal Merced – Mexico"* actually meant and I quickly found that *"Banco Banorte"* was a Mexican bank and that *"Sucursal Merced"* was in fact the name of one of its branch in Mexico City. The figures underneath were certainly some kind of account number…

*"Necessity of action takes away the fear of the act,
and makes bold resolution the favourite of fortune."*
– Francis Quarles (1592-1644)

CHAPTER 8. FEAR

Fear [noun] – an unpleasant emotion, or feeling, caused by the threat of danger, pain, or harm that is about to happen.

(Excerpt from the Storyteller Dictionary)

70. Breaking News.

Day 4 – 28th April 2009.

Summary News, UK.

The US Homeland Security Secretary said that officials at airports, land ports and border crossings in the United States have started screening travellers and questioning those who show flu-like symptoms.

Meanwhile, in Geneva, journalists were told that border screenings don't work in detecting passengers who may be infected with Swine Flu. A spokesman for the World Health Organization, based in the Swiss city, thus stressed on Tuesday that "if a person has been exposed or infected… the person might not be symptomatic at the airport. Border controls don't work. Screening doesn't work."

71. Jean Fleury.

8.30 a.m.

I woke up early in the morning so I could return to Mexico City before lunchtime and find the bank. After a quick breakfast, I went to the hotel reception to check-out. There, the same young man was inexorably playing solitaire. He barely looked at me when I returned the key but he eventually waved goodbye when I struggled in my very basic Spanish to ask him how much I had to pay for the room. I could only assume that the Aztlāns had paid for my stay.

Once I left the hotel, I found a taxi waiting outside. I just told him that I wanted to go to Mexico City and we were on our way.

Two hours later, we arrived in the capital city of Mexico. The streets there were still very much empty of people or vehicles. I gave my driver a piece of paper with the exact address of the bank, *Calle Las Cruces*. When we got there, I saw two security guards in a dark-blue uniform and wearing masks, standing in front of the bank.

My taxi stopped on the corner of the street. I went out of the car and paid the driver who made many gestures to try to help me understand his words the best he could: I realised he was actually asking me whether I wanted him to wait for me. I thought that he might have believed I was a rich American going to the bank, and he could definitely find me a way to spend some pesos in the city… I nevertheless declined his very kind offer even though he insisted three or four times.

I made my way to the entrance of the bank. I passed the automatic doors and headed straight to the reception, where a tall blond man was standing behind a desk, wearing Dolce & Gabbana silver metal rimless glasses, and a classy black Cerruti-like suit.

He looked at me without a word, not even greeting me good morning. He was just staring. That wasn't very welcoming; it was cold and quite rude of him. I knew of a bank in London where I had felt like I was a second-class customer, but this occasion beat that by far!

I took the account number out of my pocket and put it on his desk without a word. He barely looked at the paper but went to a personal bankers' computer, right behind his own desk. After typing the number on the keyboard and clicking two or three times with the mouse, he came back to me with a totally changed attitude and a very big smile on the face.

'Oh… Señor Fleury, welcome back!' he announced in pretty good English. 'My name is DeMario. What can I do for you today?'

I was about to deny being this Señor Fleury when I remembered having a key with that name on it; the key I had found in an envelope in my hotel room. I took it from my back pocket and slowly slid it on the desk towards the receptionist, who followed my gesture with his eyes and then picked up the key.

'Could you help me with that?' I asked.

'Of course. Would you like to access your safety deposit box with your usual personal banker, Señor Fleury?'

'No, don't you worry. I'm sure you'll be just fine.'

'Would you mind waiting for me for a minute? I'll ask a colleague to cover my position at the reception.'

'Take your time. I'm in no hurry…'

While the young bank receptionist was speaking to his colleagues through the cashiers' windows, asking someone to replace him so that he could take me to the bank vault, I started wandering around, between the reception and the personal bankers' desks.

That's when I accidentally saw a picture of me on the screen of the computer that the young man had just used to access Fleury's account. I discreetly came closer and realised that while the account was definitely in the name of Jean Fleury, my face was appearing there as the account's owner; it also mentioned *"VIP CUSTOMER"* with five stars. I couldn't believe that someone had actually taken the trouble to use my picture to identify me as the owner of this bank account. I decided to go on with it anyway. I thought that maybe this time, thanks to that simple key, I was going to get some answers to my questions…

DeMario came back and asked me to follow him as he headed towards the back of the room. We first passed a security door controlled by CCTVs. We then went downstairs to the basement of the bank. He scanned his badge and typed a code on a device installed on a big brown door. The door slid open very slowly. Two security guards, dressed in a similar uniform as the two I had seen outside the bank, appeared behind what looked like a huge bullet-proof door. They spoke to the bank receptionist in Spanish before I saw him identifying himself again to them and place the key on a small tray located at the bottom of the door. Then he asked me to stand still while they took a picture of me with a tiny camera.

Then they checked and probably double-checked everything on their computer, and eventually allowed us in. The door finally opened and the young man showed me the way through a very dark and cold corridor that was protected with CCTVs all the way to the vault. Once in front of the vault, he locked his badge inside another device installed beside the door and typed another code to open the door. That huge old-fashioned door was made of steel-reinforced concrete and covered in stainless steel.

When DeMario managed to unlock it, he asked me to help him pull open the incredibly thick and heavy door, while explaining that this was an early twentieth century vault and that it had been built that way so that it would be impossible to destroy. I could only agree that it would certainly be difficult to destroy such a door.

Once the door was wide open, I followed the young man inside the vault. By the door, he grabbed a folder from a small table and looked for my name; actually, Jean Fleury's.

'There we go…' he declared as he ticked a box on the sheet he had just taken from the folder. 'Your name is there, Señor Fleury. May I just ask you to sign here please?'

He let me have the folder. I suddenly had a doubt. What signature would I do? Not mine obviously. I had to invent something quickly as the young receptionist was looking at me. I then decided to simply sign *"J"* and *"F"*.

'Sorry, I never remember which signature is the right one… I use two or three different signatures at work, for banking, and for official documents…'

'It's absolutely fine, Señor.' He smiled as he took me to the safe deposit boxes. 'The signature is really just a formality anyway. If you hadn't been Jean Fleury, you would never have managed to get inside this vault, as our ultramodern computer would immediately have told the guards that something was wrong with your behaviour, or that your face didn't match the data we hold in our systems. The whole system is so secure and perfect that we haven't had a robbery since the vault was upgraded in 1981!'

So secure that someone had actually managed to get into their system to include my picture in it, so that I could access the vault… right!

DeMario turned the key in the keyhole of box 250409 from one of the top rows, grabbing it with both hands. It was a long, dark blue, steel-made box.

'Well… That's quite heavy!' He smiled again before giving me the box and making his way back to the door of the vault. 'I'll be waiting for you outside, Señor. Do not hesitate to call me if you need any help.'

'Thank you, DeMario.'

'You're welcome.'

I placed the box on a table in the centre of the room, and sat on a chair for a moment. Silence. The only noise I could hear was that of my heart beating, quicker and quicker. My hands were all sweaty, my throat was dry. It was a strange feeling, but a good feeling.

I just couldn't believe it. It had been so difficult to get there... so difficult... and so easy, in fact. Was I really going to uncover one of the secrets surrounding the Swine Flu virus origins?

72. Breaking News.

Magnus Press Agency, UK.

The United Nations' Food and Agriculture Organization (FAO) said on Tuesday that it was sending some of its animal experts to Mexico to investigate if the Swine Flu virus is really linked to pigs. "At present, transmission seems to be occurring solely from humans to humans. So far, evidence that the new strain of influenza A virus has entered the human population directly from pigs has not been established," the U.N. body said in a statement.

73. In the vault.

9.12 a.m.

I slowly and delicately opened the box. Inside, I first found a white envelope.

Yet another envelope! I thought.

I took it from the box and discovered that the only other items that were hidden there were not one, but fifteen small one-kilo gold ingots, with a market value of probably something like half a million dollars.

I just couldn't believe my eyes. What was that gold doing in this box and in this bank? What was it all about? Then I quickly noticed that each one of them had the logotype of the *Sociedad Española de Metales Preciosos* and a serial number engraved on. That seal reminded me of something that I had previously read in the little blue book… the Heathrow robbery of 1983.

I decided to let the gold aside a moment and to immediately open the envelope. Inside, I found a letter with a handwritten message.

Time to go back to London now, Mister Duprés.

Sarah is waiting for you there!

Here is a present to start a new life away from Mexico.

Enjoy!

That scary message was obviously directed to me. But how could anyone plan such a scheme, especially with what was certainly one of the most secure bank in the country, and why? Were *they* that afraid that I might have been getting too close to the truth? Who was behind it all?

The scariest part was that these people even knew about my fiancée! I needed to make sure she was safe in London. I needed to leave the vault as quickly as possible and give her a call. I was certainly not going to accept being bribed nor scared by anyone. Whoever these people were and however powerful they could be, *they* had finally shown me that there was definitely something hidden behind the official truth of the Swine Flu and my investigation wasn't in vain. And I couldn't stop thinking that I had to pursue it until the end to find out the truth.

I asked DeMario to come back to the vault while I was tidying up the contents of the box. The young man had probably noticed that I looked worried because he asked me twice if I was all right, as he was putting the box back in its space on the wall.

'I'm fine really, thank you,' I answered with a little smile. 'I just realised that I forgot to do something important, so I'll have to leave everything in the box. I won't take any of its contents now…'

'That's fine, Señor, you can always come back later or another day if you wish.'

I quickly left the bank to call Sarah in London on my iPhone as I walked down the empty street. She answered almost immediately. I started to feel relieved.

'Sarah… I'm just calling you to know if you are all right…' I stated.

'I'm ok,' she answered. 'What's going on?'

'Did you see anything strange around the house recently? Did you see or meet anyone strange, or new? Did you receive any weird phone calls?'

She now sounded a bit worried because of my call.

'Apart from your present phone call, nothing. Why?'

'Listen to me very carefully, Sarah. I want you to leave the house as soon as possible with just a bag with anything you need to wear for a few days away. I want you to take the car, take a plane, and go visit my cousin Madeleine, in Toulouse. Then you stay there for as long as I tell you to.'

'Did something go wrong during your investigation again?'

Sarah had quite obviously my previous investigation on the Iraq war in mind, when the governments of the United States and the United Kingdom had both claimed Iraq was in possession of weapons of mass destruction and was also actively supporting al-Qaeda. At the time, some obscure insiders in the British Ministry of Defence tried to set me up and get me assassinated, as I had found that there were neither WMD in Iraq nor any evidence of any connection between Saddam Hussein and al-Qaeda.

'This is different from Iraq, believe me!'

'If you say so, I believe you.'

'I can't tell you anything right now. I can only tell you that you need to leave the house now! I will contact Madeleine and let her know you're on your way. Send her a text message when you know what plane you're taking, so that she can meet you at the airport as usual. Do not call anyone. Do not speak to anyone. Just go. I'll contact you when everything is over. Ok?'

Sarah was sobbing now.

'Sarah… Please, be strong! You know everything will be all right, don't worry!'

'Please, be extremely careful with the virus as well as with your investigation!'

'I will! Je t'aime. Bye.'

'Je t'aime, Jean-Baptiste.'

74. Breaking News.

The Custodian, UK.

"The Swine Flu can no longer be contained as the virus has spread to Asia and the Middle East," the World Health Organization (WHO) warned today. About 2,000 people are believed to be infected in the country, while the number of cases in the USA doubled and

Britain confirmed its first case. First infections are also confirmed in Israel and New Zealand, while Spain confirmed a second case today and South Korea said they had a "probable" case.

In the meantime, the Foreign Office has been advising British citizens in Mexico "to consider whether they should remain there". Schools are now closed across Mexico. And the death toll in Mexico rose to 152.

75. Threat.

9.47 a.m.

As I finished my call, I received three mysterious text messages.

Unknown sender: Your investigation has to stop. Otherwise you won't get to be old…

Unknown sender: If you keep going with your investigation, some accident could occur…

Unknown sender: Whatever happens in the world today… it had to happen!

These three messages had undoubtedly the same origin and had certainly not been sent to me just by chance as I was leaving the bank without the gold. I wasn't even going to bother wondering how *they* had managed to get my mobile phone number, as I now knew *they* knew a lot more about me than I first thought, and that *they* were able to do anything. There was no doubt in my mind that the sender of these messages definitely knew that I had refused their gold.

I often heard people say that everyone has a price. Well, I didn't. I had honourable principles and as a journalist, I also had ethics. So I really couldn't care less about their offer.

76. Breaking News.

The Impartial Newspaper, UK.

Are people in Mexico City simply hiding or are they preparing for the apocalypse? Schools, cinemas, museums, restaurants, bars, and other public places have all been ordered to close by the Mexican government. It has also advised "those who could avoid it not to go to work." About seventy percent of all restaurants and bars in the capital were actually closed over the weekend.

Quite an apocalyptic vision that is, however, tempered by the "business as usual" in some public places, such as La Merced Market, the largest retail traditional food market in Mexico, located in the historic centre of the city.

77. At the market.

11.28 a.m.

First, *they* chased me. Then *they* tried to kill me. As I always managed to escape from them, *they* tried bribing me. The bribe didn't work, so *they* came back to basics and threatened me again. But who were *they*?

I was going to look for a new hotel to stay in the capital for a few days, when I suddenly received another text message on my iPhone.

Unknown sender: Meet me at Mercado de la Merced at 12 p.m., by the butchers' stalls. Please, don't be late! DoctorVanity1918

At least this time, I knew who the sender was. My contact wanted to meet me at what was Mexico City's biggest market and certainly one of the most fascinating in the whole country. From the bank, I was about ten minutes' walk away. On my way, I took the occasion to post the DNA sample from the little boy in Cholula to my scientifist friend in London.

When I arrived at the market, I firstly noticed the stalls lining up in the crowded streets leading to the market, selling food, drinks, clothes, and CDs and DVDs… Then I arrived in front of a huge light-yellow building that held the actual market. The sight of it kept me absolutely gobsmacked for a while. That building was actually made of several huge buildings and the whole thing was about half a kilometre long. According to what Pedro had told me, it would take at least half an hour to go from the north entrances to the south. There were literally people, colours, signs, items and stalls everywhere, inside and outside the building. Two police officers were also there, keeping an eye on everything, while some soldiers were busy trying to distribute masks to the visitors, who barely wanted them.

The level of activity there was still pretty intense just as if nothing was happening in the country, as if there wasn't any virus at all. Only the presence of the soldiers reminded everyone about the Swine Flu, otherwise, it was as if the show had to go on anyway.

I set foot in the *"fiesta market"* as Pedro used to call it, and went through its narrow corridors, one by one, looking for the butchers' stalls. In the first building, there were some extremely tidy stalls with pyramids of very shiny and colourful fruits and vegetables, then came the spices with every shade of green, orange, yellow, and red chillies you could imagine. The smell of fish and seafood were next. Being a real aficionado of seafood, and a bit early for my rendezvous, I spent some time looking at what the traders had to offer: some crabs, lovely prawns, mojarra fishes, octopuses, and lots of other seafood.

When I eventually found the butchers, I thought that I was visiting a public slaughterhouse with chickens, heads, shoulders, legs, and all other pieces of cows and pigs hanging everywhere in the building. The stalls were also displaying raw minced meat and sausages, as well as grilled, fried, cooked, seasoned and preserved meat and hams. All the food display looked quite cheap and unhygienic, with hundreds of flies buzzing around touching unclean surfaces, standing water, but also fishes, poultry, and cattle. It was so hot in the city and so hot in this building that I was really wondering how the food didn't contain any salmonella.

Suddenly I felt a small hand weighing on my right shoulder. I turned around and immediately recognised my contact, *DoctorVanity1918*. She was really pretty in her light blue summer dress that was showing off her slim figure, her curves, and her long legs. She was also wearing some very discreet make-up and holding a small blue purse in her hands, and a small light-blue umbrella.

'I love this market, I really do,' she announced with a big smile. 'Good morning, Jean-Baptiste… You know, I used to come here with my parents when I was a child. I always loved the smells and the variety of the food available, the fantastic people we can meet on every corner, and the great atmosphere all together.'

'Good morning to you too,' I replied, while she led the way across the corridors. 'It certainly is a nice place, but I'm quite surprised that the market stayed open despite the virus outbreak.'

'What you see here today isn't even half of what this market is all about. Very many traders didn't show up this morning because of their fear of the Swine Flu. The number of visitors is also very far from what I would expect on a Tuesday morning. But as you can see, there are still people coming to work and coming to buy. That's something very Mexican, you know, to be able to go on with life even though a calamity has just struck.

'With the economic crisis first, then the virus, and the earthquake yesterday, some people simply feel like it's the Apocalypse. I understand them, I understand their fear. It's normal. It's human. These people are so scared, they would rather hide at home than face the reality and fight, but there are others like these traders who think that life must go on, because fighting for survival is part of our culture. It's part of who we are deep inside.'

'Through your words, I think you're very proud to be Mexican, aren't you?'

'Indeed I am.'

We passed in front of stalls displaying enormous pigs' heads that nobody seemed to want to buy. The butchers there looked really frustrated by the situation.

She unexpectedly pulled me over to a less crowded corner and stayed still a moment. She then came closer to me, looking directly in my eyes. She came so close that I could detect her usual smell of vanilla again. Her delicate pink lips were slightly glossy and smelt of strawberries. I wasn't too comfortable with this closeness. On the contrary, she looked very confident. Her nose grazed mine as she whispered something in my ear.

'Jean-Baptiste, I asked you to meet me here today for a simple reason,' she whispered, giving me a sensual kiss on the cheek. 'For I am going to tell you everything you wanted to know about me…'

I couldn't understand her sudden strange change of behaviour towards me. Was she actually trying to seduce me?

'Come on, kiss me, now!' she ordered, holding my head between her hands and staring into my eyes in an extremely serious way.

'What?... But, wait…'

78. Breaking News.

La Presencia, MEXICO.
Jesús Lorenzano's Blog.

So, I think that the Swine Flu is nothing but the fourth plague! We had to go through a financial crisis, an economic crisis, and a social crisis, and these three aren't even finished yet!

Who will suffer the most from the new epidemic? The poorest! Our country, our institutions, our government, our financial system, our administration, they have all been very unhealthy for quite a long time now. Unfortunately, this condition is killing more and more Mexicans every day all over the country, and nothing seems to be able to stop it!

79. The kiss.

12.12 p.m.

'Listen. There are two men dressed in black by the entrance of the butchers' building,' she explained in my ear. 'The only way to avoid them seeing us right now is if we kiss. So don't start stammering, just kiss me!'

So we kissed.

*"Revenge is the naked idol
of the worship of a semi-barbarous age."*
– Percy Bysshe Shelley (1792 – 1822)

CHAPTER 9. FAKE

Fake [verb] – to forge or counterfeit something to make
it appear real, or more valuable, by fraud.

(Excerpt from the Storyteller Dictionary)

80. The Library.

12.13 p.m.

Our kiss lasted at least a minute or maybe even two. I wouldn't say that it wasn't pleasant to kiss her because, to be honest it was, but the circumstances of the kiss weren't the most enjoyable. Besides, I couldn't stop thinking about Sarah, who would have killed me quicker than the men in black had wanted to if she had seen us kissing. But it was a very innocent kiss, lips against lips, without any feeling. In a way, I could even say that it was a kiss of life, because we did manage to escape the bald men. Well, did I need to justify myself in any way?

When we stopped kissing, the young woman discreetly turned her head to see if the men in black were still around. They had gone. She then turned back to me and finally introduced herself.

'I'm Alicia Thomson by the way. And just in case you still have a doubt, that's my real name.'

We smiled at each other. It was funny that I finally got to know her name only after we had kissed. She gave me a mask before putting on her own, then took my hand and asked me to follow her.

'An English name?' I asked as we left the building by the side door. 'How come?'

Moving between more traders and stalls, avoiding foods and other items on our way, we eventually made it to the outside where there were all kinds of vans and cars parked all along the street. These were the traders' vehicles.

Alicia opened her light-blue umbrella to protect us from the sun, but also to avoid any suspicions from whoever was looking for us. We walked down Calle Rosario, hand-in-hand like lovers do, but wearing surgical masks like everybody else in the street.

'I was born in Tlaxcala, twenty-five years ago. My mother was Mexican while my father's parents were English. That explains my name…'

'…and your fluency in English too,' I added.

She winked at me.

'My father's career in the Mexican Air Force took our family to different cities in Mexico, such as Cozumel, El Ciprés, and Ixtepec before settling in the state of Mexico in Santa Lucía, when I was nine years old. My family was a very conservative, traditional, Catholic Latin-American family, but my older brother and I actually grew up to be very liberal.'

The young woman, who had something of Jessica Alba in her face, was without a doubt very beautiful, and very confident. Her ways were naturally smooth. You could also easily tell that she was very clever and ingenious. But there was something else about her that I couldn't really describe, something that made her different from any other woman I had met.

'After I graduated from the *Universidad Nacional Autónoma de México* at eighteen, the university offered me work at the *Institute of Anthropological Research.* They had a *Multidisciplinary Research Programme on Mesoamerica and the South East.* They wanted me to become a specialist of Mesoamerica, which is the study of the most complex and advanced cultures and ancient civilisations of the Americas, such as the Olmecs, the Teotihuacans, the Mixtecs, the Zapotecs, the Mayas, and the Mexicas.'

'I understand now why the little blue book was so accurate about the Mexicas and the Spanish Conquest! Although I thought you told me online that you were actually working for a pharmaceutical company...'

'You were looking for answers about the virus. Would you have seriously listened to me if I told you that I was a specialist of Mesoamerica? I don't think so! Sorry that I had to lie to you, but I didn't have much choice.'

'Point taken.'

'I worked for the Institute for five years. My job involved the decryption and cataloguing of the Mexicas' Codices that have been spread all over the world since the Spanish Conquest,' she continued. 'That also included finding the supposedly lost or destroyed codices. Then I was supposed to make my work available to the wide public by publishing my findings on the University's anthropology webpage.'

'You're talking in the past tense. Did something bad happen?'

'Well, yes. During my research, I came across a few fake codices, among which was the most important one, the Vatican's.'

'I remember the little blue book mentioning that two codices were found among Cardinal Stefano's belongings,' I agreed.

The temperature in Mexico was almost unbearable at more than 40° Celsius. We turned into a less crowded street where we found just a dozen stalls, as many vans, two or three cars, and only a few people, also wearing masks. Then in the corner of that street, Alicia got rid of the umbrella and opened the door of a small silver Fiat 500 parked in front of a butcher's shop. I quickly stepped into the car with her and while the engine was warming up, she continued her story.

'So the Vatican Library had two Codices Borgia in its possession. When I visited the Library in Rome, in June 2007, they allowed me to examine both codices. The first codex was an authentic account of historical as well as legendary events of what we call the *"Early Postclassic"* period of Mesoamerica. Whereas the second codex I examined was an obvious gross replica of a lost codex that I had discovered six months earlier, inside an ancient Christian monastery in Maalula, Syria.'

'Did they really think they would ever deceive the experts?'

'I think so! As I knew it was a fake, at the end of my work session in the Library, I met with some of the senior management. I first met the *Vice-Prefect* at the reception desk, who denied my findings. Then it was the *Prefect* in a corridor of the Library, who also denied that the second codex was a fake. As I was really persistent, I finally got to meet with the *Librarian of the Roman Catholic Church*, in his office. He also insisted that my findings were certainly not accurate, and that the likelihood for any document available at the Vatican Library being a fake was not only zero but, and I quote him, it was also *"Utterly unimaginable, unthinkable, and inconceivable."*

'When I explained that I was a specialist of Mesoamerica at the University of Mexico, he simply repudiated my expertise due to, and once again I quote him, my *"Young age, indisputable inexperience, and total immaturity."'*

The car started moving. Alicia was driving very slowly to avoid some traders who were still crossing the street with their wheelbarrows full of items to sell.

'He simply wouldn't let me explain my arguments that proved the codex was a fake. He simply wouldn't listen. So I ended the conversation telling him that I was going to publish my findings online anyway, and that maybe then other experts, older and more experienced than I, would decide to have a look at it and would come to the same conclusion. The moment I said that, his behaviour changed for the worst. He threatened to have me banned from the Library for life if my study talked about the codex and explicitly claimed that it was a fake. He argued that such an allegation would start a media frenzy and bring some very bad publicity to the church; it would take the Vatican into an unjustified battle of experts, with all kinds of old clichés and old accusations re-emerging, and it would definitely put the Holy See and the world in great turmoil. He finished his speech by saying that I had a very important decision to make and that choosing to publish my study would mean the end of my career and would bring hell to Earth!'

'What did you do then?' I asked, looking at her beautiful emerald green eyes.

'Back in Mexico, I simply did what I had to do as an expert of Mesoamerica. I published my work online.'

'What happened next?'

'A few hours after my six-hundred-page essay was published on the university website, and republished on diverse other scientific websites, a colleague from a university in Italy contacted me by email to say that the Vatican had just announced that its Library was to be shut for at least three years for what they said was important rebuilding works. My colleague also added that as far as he knew, the Library had never been closed for so long before in its five-century history. I thought it was a very interesting coincidence!'

81. Archives.

New York Chimes, USA. (June 2007)

The Vatican has recently announced that the Vatican Library is to close in July for a three-year renovation. The Vatican Library has one of the most important manuscript collections in the world, along with the National Library of France and the British Library.

Since the announcement, visiting scholars from everywhere in the world have been queuing up every day to be able to grab a seat in the Manuscript Room, where only 92 seats are available, to read ancient texts in every languages of the planet. Their fear is to be cut off from their main source of information as many of them have research on the way.

82. Who is Alicia?

12.38 p.m.

The men in black didn't seem to have found us, but we had to remain vigilante. That's why Alicia was driving us to her former place of work, the Institute of Anthropological Research, a thirty-five-minute ride towards the south of the capital, where she told me one colleague would be able to provide us with a safe haven for a few days.

'The next day, I received a strange phone call from a man saying he was working for a big company and his boss was interested in meeting me with a job offer. So I went to the company's head office in the north of the city and there I met a man called Rodrigo Stefano Borgia Anzules.'

'The man from the book, I presume?'

'That very man!'

She explained that the Guatemalan multi-billionaire had first told her about his great passion for antiques and about his private collection in New York, before explaining he had heard of her after the chaos her essay about the Mexicas' codices and the fake Vatican codex had generated. He had added that, to him, her name was synonymous with integrity and that he needed someone like her to help run one of his foundations. He had thus offered her to join his team of experts and scientists, to discover where the real mysterious Codex was and to understand its meaning.

'I was given carte-blanche on the project and would be offered all relevant information to help me find the Codex, through the most comprehensive data files ever collected on the Mexicas' codices and on the Vatican: the *Aztlān Project Foundation*'s! The offer was so appealing that I couldn't refuse, so I immediately signed the contract.'

'Wait… What does the *Aztlān Project* have to do with Anzules and his foundation?' I asked, looking at the streets still so empty of cars. 'Is he involved with them?'

'Indirectly, yes. You see, Anzules was a man on a mission with a master plan. His plan B was to incriminate the real Aztlān Project organisation if his master plan was to fail, so that no one would ever come to suspect him of any wrongdoing.'

'Incriminate them for doing what?' I asked, thinking the story was getting more and more sinister. 'What was his master plan?'

'Last December, I was visiting Anzules in his New York headquarters one evening, to tell him that I was planning on returning to Rome to investigate the lost Codex at the Vatican. While I was waiting for him in another room, I overheard some bits of a phone conversation he was having. I heard him saying things like, *"Tell them I'm really not joking! We know now that they only ever exposed the fake one! If they don't give me the damn Codex and the gold, I'll let the virus out! Tell them it's the Codex and the gold against the virus! Millions of lives are now in their bloody hands!"* He wasn't joking!'

'Was he then talking about the virus? The Swine Flu virus?...'

'He was indeed!'

'Wait, Alicia, are you telling me that the virus was actually created by Anzules? Why?'

She explained that Rodrigo Anzules had always been passionate about Mexicas antiques. But he also always had a lot of resentment regarding his heritage. When he was fifteen, he had accidently discovered his ancestor's notes in a box that had been secretly kept inside a wall at his grandparents' house for generations. Thanks to that box, he had access to a lot of information regarding the Vatican, the Mexicas, and the hidden gold; all except where the gold actually was. Among the hundreds of notes in the box, there was one that Stefano Borgia had written saying that even though he hadn't told anyone about the codices, he still feared for his life. It went on to say that if no other note was to be written by him after that, one had to assume that the other Cardinals had probably had him assassinated to take possession of the two codices. He was indeed assassinated and all his properties taken by the Vatican.

'From the day he found that secret box, the young Anzules was always aiming for revenge on the Vatican for his ancestor and for his family,' she claimed, as we smoothly changed lanes. 'Anzules has built his entire life, his businesses, and his fortune, keeping in mind that one day he would definitely avenge Stefano Borgia. You must understand one very important thing, Jean-Baptiste, Rodrigo Anzules was and always is a man on a mission, and he will not let anything or anyone get in his way! Believe me!'

'How do you know so many things about it?' I asked. I noticed we were passing near the capital's Olympic Stadium. 'How do you even know so many details about Anzules himself?'

Alicia turned to me, pushed her hair off her face, and calmly answered me.

'Quite simply, I'm his wife!'

*"Three things cannot be long hidden:
the sun, the moon, and the truth."*
– Siddhārtha Gautama Buddha (563 BC – 483 BC)

CHAPTER 10. THE TRUTH

Truth [noun] – something that has the quality or state of being true, genuine, or factual.

(Excerpt from the Storyteller Dictionary)

83. Stephano Borgia's secret diary.

23th November 1804.

Even though I haven't told anyone about the Codices, not even *In Pectore*, I have recently felt like somebody was spying on me. I don't know who they are, but I can only think they work for the Cardinals, who want more than anything to take over the codices.

I must say I really think my life is now at risk. That's the reason why I declare today that if I don't write any new notes in this diary from tomorrow, one should only assume that the Cardinals will have had me assassinated.

The hidden gold stolen was certainly not enough to them, especially since none of us has ever seen it or used it!

84. Breaking News.

The Health of the World, SWITZERLAND.

Seven countries have now reported cases of Swine Flu in the world. According to the World Health Organization (WHO), Mexico has reported 26 confirmed cases and seven deaths. The United States have reported 64 confirmed cases, no deaths.

The WHO "does not advise any restrictions of travel or closure of borders" and confirms that "there is no risk of infection from consumption of well-cooked pork and pork products." Everyone is also reminded that the best way to fight the virus is still to regularly wash their hands thoroughly with soap and water.

85. The virus.

1.02 p.m.

'His wife?' I repeated, literally gobsmacked.

'His wife!' she repeated, passing a blue sign with yellow text saying *"Centro Cultural Universitário"*, which meant we were slowly getting to our destination.

'Over the years, Anzules built a very strong reputation as an entrepreneur, but he is also quite well-known for his charming ways,' she explained, trying to justify why she was the multibillionaire's wife. 'I have to admit that I fell for him and his sweet words whispered in my ears. But I now realise that I was barely a pawn in his game. He needed me to take him to the Codex and the gold, and he would have done anything to help me succeed in my enterprise, even if that meant seducing me and marrying me! So we got married a little more than two years ago, in September 2007, and we still are, unfortunately! The good side of the story – if there is one actually – is that, like every self-made man in the world, he told me a lot about him during the long evenings we spent together. He told me so much that I could write a biography about him!'

As we arrived at the building of the *Institute of Anthropological Research*, I asked her what made her realise who Anzules really was.

'I must say that a thought definitely struck me on that evening in New York, last December, when I overheard his conversation about the virus. I suddenly understood that something was wrong with him, that he wasn't the gentleman I had thought he was, and that he was even quite a dangerous man. It really was a wake-up call. I then started my own investigation within his circle of trust and his company, and pretty easily I found all kind of documents relating to the virus and his *master plan*.'

I still didn't know what Anzules' *master plan* was, but as she was parking the car in the Institute's car park, she finally explained it to me.

'His master plan was to threaten the Vatican's *In Pectore* so the Cardinals would submit to his authority and give him the remaining Jaca gold that they were still in possession of, as well as the precious Codex that once belonged to his ancestors. He already had a go at them once before in 1983, with the famous robbery at Heathrow airport, which is mentioned in the book. It was a robbery that he had secretly financed to prove to the Cardinals that he knew a lot about their business and he was serious about his demands. But they categorically refused his blackmail. Threatening was one thing, acting on it was different. So he upgraded his threat and told them that unless they took him more seriously, he would release a brand new virus that had the phenomenal capability of targeting and eliminating one particular population in the world…'

'How did he create such a virus?' I naively asked.

'Anzules owns many companies in America, and among them, a big pharmaceutical company called *Borgia Labs Inc*. In 2001, after the attack on the World Trade Center and the invasion of Afghanistan, *Borgia Labs* received an order from the US Government. The Pentagon wanted them to create a new biological weapon they could use against enemies during conflicts, but also on civilians, without leaving any trace behind. In their presentation, they even suggested a virus to control and shrink the world's population. The lab thus worked on different virus projects and eventually offered the Pentagon a brand new virus they called *H1N1-GTV*. It was a virus that could target one particular genetic background, one particular population. That's why they called it a *GTV, a gene targeted virus*. But after major budget cuts, the Pentagon rejected the offer and simply cancelled the order.'

'So the Swine Flu virus was in fact originally designed for the US Government?'

'Yes, but it's Anzules who ended up by benefiting the most from the newly created virus. As he still needed to prove to the Cardinals that he was serious about his demands, he ordered that the virus be injected into the pigs of a farm that belonged to him. It had to be discreet and effortless. His men even contacted a few experts from the World Health Organization and got them to agree with his plan to launch the virus in a small Mexican town called Santa Isabel Cholula.'

'Why there?'

'In 1519, Hernán Cortés, in a pre-meditated effort to inspire fear upon the Mexicas who were waiting for him in Tenochtitlan, conducted a wicked massacre there. The Spaniards killed thousands of unarmed people and partially burned down the city... Anzules simply wanted to do the same to inspire fear upon the Aztlāns and the Cardinals.'

'Wow!'

'The farm, called *Granja Dodgson*, belonged to a company called Virginia Foods, which itself belonged to Anzules Group. The virus was to target only Tlaxcalan descendants for now, as a warning to the Vatican. It worked pretty well, as you can see. The virus is effective and spreads quickly around the world. If I was one of the Cardinals, I would really be scared now!'

We got out of the car and closed our doors.

'After having created the virus, *Borgia Labs* worked on antiviral drugs and also created *Sanniflu*, which is very well-known in the industry for being quite dangerous for the patients, because of its possible side-effects, including delirium, hallucinations, or suicidal behaviour...'

I couldn't believe I was learning so many things about the Swine Flu virus in such a short period of time. My investigation had never moved forward so much since I started it.

We were making our way to the main building of the institute when six men in black suddenly appeared in front of us, then three black cars also arrived behind us, with many more bald men getting out of the cars and moving rapidly towards us.

Time to make a decision.

86. Archives.

Health of the World, UK. (February 2006)

Corruption is killing our health too. According to a just-released encyclopaedic report into corruption, in every country of the world, the health systems are exposed to corruption from the governments to the patients. About 100,000 pharmaceutical representatives ply doctors with gifts, free meals, events, and sprees, in the US, for a total cost of US$ 2 billion per year. A famous example: the decision taken by the US Food and Drug Administration (FDA) to keep the drugs Vidii and Vicii on the market, even though there were concerns that they could increase cardiovascular risk. But *The Health of the World* later found out that most of the panellists of the FDA committee had financial ties to the laboratory.

If these experts had not voted, the decision would have gone the other way!

87. Run!

1.33 p.m.

'Run!' I screamed to Alicia, as one man was about to grab her arm. 'Run!'

She managed to escape and gave the man a well-deserved kick in the face. The others ran after us. While the three cars returned to the main road outside the institute fence to try and stop us, Alicia was leading the way, running toward some gigantic colourful sculptures in the park surrounding the university.

The grass and bushes were slowing us down, but the young woman really seemed to know where to go to escape to our pursuers. At some point, it actually even looked like we had managed to lose them as there was no one behind us. It seemed too easy though. We went near a long small brick wall, some kind of ruin that was crossing the park, where Alicia told me the best thing to do was to split up so that the men in black wouldn't catch us together. We ran again together for a while though, with still no sign of anyone following us.

'Jean-Baptiste, I've got all the documents proving everything I've just told you about Anzules,' she claimed, breathless, as we finally had a rest behind a big orange sculpture. 'But if they catch us together, we will never be able to get anyone to believe the story!'

'What if they catch you? How will I ever prove anything on my own without any of these documents?' I asked worriedly, keeping an eye on the bushes and trees around us.

'A friend at the institute has been keeping all the documents in a safe place for me since the first day I contacted you on the Internet. Her name is Claudia. If something happens to me, she will contact you by email.'

From a distance, I could see three men in black looking for us, and waving their guns in all directions around them. But they were still quite far and eventually decided to move to the opposite direction after one of their colleagues called them there.

'Why did you not simply send these documents to the authorities?' I questioned Alicia.

'For the very simple reason that too many people at various levels within the Mexican local and federal governments are involved in the virus story. These people have been corrupted by Anzules to cover up the story.'

'Why am I not surprised?' I stated rhetorically.

'Believe me when I say that Anzules is extremely powerful. When you leave Mexico, you'll see that all the media on the planet only talk about the Swine Flu as an extremely dangerous and contagious virus, but no one except you is actually asking where it came from. It's just as if nobody really cares that a virus suddenly emerged from nowhere and started killing everyone.'

We moved around the sculpture slightly so we could still see the men in black without being spotted ourselves. Alicia explained that, through the virus, Anzules was showing the Cardinals that he wasn't just a man of words; he could really strike whenever and wherever he wanted to. Besides, he was also making a huge profit out of the situation by selling the dangerous Sanniflu in huge quantities all over the world through his company. She claimed that he had even managed to get the World Health Organization, which some of his men had infiltrated during the last decade, to recommend Sanniflu as the unique answer to the spread of the virus.

Alicia also claimed that Anzules' men were working so hard at the WHO, lobbying and offering bribes, that they could quite easily make the organisation take the decision to raise the level to pandemic within a few days only. She finally added that a certain number of members of the WHO board, advisors on vaccines, and members of the WHO group *"Strategic Advisory Group of Experts"* (SAGE), had recently received millions of Euros for their research centres from Anzules' vaccine manufacturer.

I was at the same time both puzzled and terrified to hear that Anzules had such power that he could even influence the World Health Organization's decision on medicines and virus threat levels. Was there anything or anyone on Earth that hadn't been bought, infiltrated, or corrupted by that hideous man?

88. Archives.

Health of the World, UK. (January 2009)

Have you ever heard about the SAGE? SAGE stands for Strategic Advisory Group of Experts on Immunization. It was created in 1999 by the World Health Organization to offer information on the work of the WHO Immunization, Vaccines, and Biological Department. It is the main consultative group to the WHO for vaccines and immunization, advising the UN body on overall global policies and strategies. SAGE's members are recognized experts with outstanding records of achievements in their own field. They are appointed by the Director-General of WHOM, following recommendations from an external selection panel.

89. The lioness.

1.51 p.m.

Alicia and I eventually split, wishing each other good luck.

'If we both manage to get out of here, let's meet at 6 p.m. at the International Airport, Terminal 1, by Domino's Pizza?'

'All right.'

'Good luck, Jean-Baptiste!' she told me before kissing me on the lips.

This time it was a quick kiss, nothing to do with what had happened at the market earlier. It was actually pretty strange to think that we only kissed when our enemies were chasing us. As far as I was concerned, I couldn't hide the fact that I was really starting to like the girl. But splitting then was probably for the best.

So she went her way, and I went mine. After walking for two or three minutes along a dense wall of bushes, I suddenly heard two voices. I stopped. Two men in black were hiding right on the other side of the bushes, smoking and speaking in Spanish.

Then I heard a woman's voice. She was screaming in Spanish. I wasn't absolutely sure if it was Alicia, but when I heard the two men moving away, I had a closer look through the bush and saw five men trying to restrain Alicia on the grass.

They were now seven, holding her face down with their guns pointing at her. They quickly put some tape around her mouth to stop her screaming. She was fighting like a lioness trying to escape her captors, giving kicks and punches to everyone, until one man eventually hit her on the head with the stock of his gun. They then easily carried her limp body to one of their vehicles waiting further down the road.

I felt absolutely useless at the scene. I couldn't do anything to prevent them from taking her away unless I wanted to get killed. They were seven men with guns, I was alone and unarmed. This situation reminded me of the Basilica with Pedro, except that this time Alicia was only unconscious, not dead. I thought that if I was to stop a car on the road and make it follow them, I would have time enough to think of a plan to rescue her.

All the men jumped into the cars before the gang vanished with Alicia on board. As I was leaving the bushes to run to the road, something very heavy pushed me back down to the grass. I literally fell on the grass like a large piece of meat in a slaughterhouse. I turned my head to see my *friend* Carlos, lying on my back and keeping me from standing up.

'Don't you dare move, Jean-Baptiste!' he whispered in my right ear.

90. How about…

2.08 p.m.

'If you want to live, my friend, don't move!' Carlos added as the cars left the university campus with Alicia as their prisoner.

So I didn't ask anything and just stayed there, still and quiet. I then understood that Carlos had probably just saved my life when another car that was moving very slowly on the road, far behind the other cars, suddenly left too. There was no doubt that if I had been up and running after Alicia's kidnappers, the men in the last car would have shot me in the back.

Once the car was far enough away that I wouldn't be seen, Carlos helped me stand up. As I was cleaning my T-shirt and my jeans, full of grass, he unexpectedly punched me right in the face. I was so surprised by this sudden assault that it took me a few seconds before I realised what had just happened. I noticed that my lips were slightly bleeding as I cleaned them with my right hand.

'What was that for?' I demanded.

'That was for you not being careful enough and almost getting yourself killed!' Carlos answered in a very upset voice.

'What are you talking about?'

Carlos looked very angry. His eyes were like fire and I wouldn't have bet whether he was going to hit me again. I simply stepped back before demanding more answers.

'Why did you punch me? What did I do?'

'I'm talking about you suddenly leaving the hotel in Tlaxcala, then going to Cholula, going to the farm, and finally coming back to Mexico. You were basically showing yourself to the world and to the bad guys, despite the fact I told you we were going to look after you and the best thing for you to do was to keep a low profile for a while…'

'How do you know I went to Cholula? And how did you know I was here now? Have you been following me?'

'Of course we've been following you!' insisted Carlos, looking up at the sky. 'Our organisation needs you. Our organisation is secret and so are our activities. The authorities chase us, the army chase us. We cannot trust anyone. But since the beginning of your investigation, you showed us you are open-minded and you share our belief that the truth has to prevail. You are our messenger.'

I was listening quietly. I wanted to know what it I had that others didn't that made me so special in their eyes.

'Jean-Baptiste, do you remember our investigation in Guantanamo Bay? Do you remember how difficult it was to bring to light that story about the detainees being tortured? Who was to be blamed for not letting the truth being known back then? The military! Well, believe me or not, in this country, it's pretty much the same. The Mexican authorities, the police, or the military, they are all not to be trusted. They will use you as much as they can to get what they want. Most of them work for Rodrigo Anzules, a very rich man who wants our organisation destroyed and our members dead. The others have either been bribed by that man. Or are already dead! In Mexico, there is no one you can trust but yourself. In Mexico, you don't have friends or enemies, you have only enemies. If you have any friends, they will soon become your closest enemies and, sometimes, they will even ally with your other enemies.'

Carlos asked me to follow him to his car. We then walked for a little bit.

'I know that you have met Anzules' wife, Alicia. I also know that she has been in contact with you throughout your investigation and that she has been helping you a lot with the understanding of the situation with the virus, our organisation, the Vatican, and Anzules. But you must also understand that she has put her life in danger by doing so. My little sister is a brave girl, but she's still very young too! Now, she's Anzules' prisoner again; you and I are going to go and rescue her today. Then I'll tell you more about Anzules…'

We crossed the park again and came back to the place Alicia and I had left our car. There, Sergio seemed to be sleeping deeply at the wheel. Carlos gave a loud slap onto the roof of the car and Sergio abruptly woke up with a jump.

'¡Vamos, Sergio, vamos!' he shouted, letting the big man know that it was time for him to move away from the wheel.

But when Carlos opened the door of the car, Sergio didn't move. I was about to get into the car myself, but I had a strange feeling and decided to stay outside for the moment. Sergio slowly turned to Carlos with that big daft smile he used on occasions. But his smile slowly changed into a dirty look with the same rage in his eyes and bared teeth as a wolf would have when about to catch his prey.

All of a sudden, Sergio jumped onto Carlos, screaming things in Spanish, and both men fell on the macadam. He started punching Carlos like a boxer and before I could do anything, Carlos' face was already bleeding profusely. I grabbed a piece of wood being used as a tree trellis in the institute gardens, and I hit the colossus twice on the back with it. The third time, the wood broke and Sergio finally stopped beating up poor Carlos to actually turn his head, look at me, and walk slowly towards me.

With my miserable broken piece of wood in hand, I thought that I was going to die from being beaten up by the giant man. I was waiting for judgement day, when Sergio spoke to me in perfect English.

'How about you come with me now to meet Señor Anzules?'

Then he knocked me out.

91. Breaking News.

USNN News International, USA.

The World Health Organization raised its pandemic alert level to five on Wednesday. The important decision to raise the alert means, "All countries of the world should immediately activate pandemic preparedness plans," said the agency's director-general. The number of confirmed cases has recently significantly increased across the world, with 148 confirmed cases in nine countries. More than 2,700 patients worldwide are believed to be suffering from Swine Flu.

Mexico counts seven deaths and the United States one. Because of the outbreak, the Mexican authorities have already ordered about 35,000 public venues in the capital city to shut down. As for the restaurants, they can only serve take-out meals. Mexico's health secretary announced on Wednesday, "All non-essential government offices and private business have been ordered to close from May 1st to 5th." What about the economic impact of the virus on the country? Mexican officials said it was far too early to quantify it.

The Custodian, UK.

Even the British Museum's Aztec exhibition that is to
take place in September, dedicated to the Aztec ruler
Moctezuma II, is now being threatened by the Swine Flu.
"The artefacts due to be exhibited in London are stuck
in the Mexican museums that are lending them to the
British Museum," explained the director and
exhibition's curator, who has just returned from Mexico
City. "The reason for that is pretty simple: the
museums there are all closed!" The British Museum will
now be closely monitoring the situation.

92. In a sentimental mood.

Day 5 – 29th April 2009, 7.08 p.m.

I regained consciousness in a very dark room. I was lying on the
floor, my hands and feet were bound together just like an animal. My
mouth and my head were quite painful, certainly because of Carlos' punch
and Sergio's knockout. I couldn't really see anything in the room, just
some light passing through the keyhole of what I assumed was a door,
located somewhere opposite me.

I could, however, hear some kind of jazz music. After paying
attention, I recognised one of my favourite songs, *"In a Sentimental
Mood"*, by one of my favourite jazz musicians, Arturo O'Farrill. It
sounded definitely more *live* than as if it was coming from a CD player,
especially when I heard the cheers of an audience, and then another song
being played.

I didn't have a clue where I was, but I had the feeling that I wasn't
in Mexico City any longer. The door opened suddenly, flashing a harsh
light from another room into my eyes, and some individuals grabbed me by
the arms to take me somewhere else. The light was so strong that I had to
keep my eyes shut while I was being moved from my room, taken up the

stairs, and finally forced to sit on a really uncomfortable wooden chair, which I was immediately tied to. In this room, the music was much louder.

'Good evening, Mister Duprés!' said a very deep voice in front of me.

I eventually managed to open my eyes to see a bald man in his thirties, dressed in a black suit and white tie, sitting behind a desk right in front of me, with six bodyguards around him.

'My name is Rodrigo Stefano Borgia Anzules,' he added with a smile. 'But I'm sure you know me better as Rodrigo Anzules, or even more simply, Anzules, thanks to the little blue book written by my beloved wife, Alicia!'

93. Archives.

ThatsYourJazz.com, USA. (April 2009)

Do not miss the 2009 Grammy Award winning artist, Arturo O'Farrill Solo, at the Muppets Jazz Bar for an hour of pure jazz, on Wednesday, Apr 29, at 7:00 p.m. It will only cost you $10 with a 2-item minimum purchase.

94. In cold blood.

7.19 p.m.

'Where are we?' I asked.

Anzules motioned one of his men, who came over to me and relentlessly punched me in the stomach. It wasn't as painful as Sergio's beating, but it was bad enough.

'I ask the questions here, Mister Duprés!' Anzules insisted.

The music was still playing in the background and I suddenly realised that, I could actually see Arturo O'Farrill playing downstairs through a large two-way mirror on my left. It was somewhat funny to think that the day I finally had the chance to see my favourite musician on stage was the day I was kidnapped by Anzules' men.

'You are such a resilient man, I must say! My boys have tried to get rid of you on numerous occasions, but without success. Then when I realised how stubborn and determined you are, I offered you a way out for a better life with your English fiancée. But there, once again, you refused my tempting offer and tenaciously insisted on continuing with this bloody investigation of yours! Can you tell me what it is that drives you so hard in this matter?'

I looked at the man who was literally behaving like a pasha, or more precisely, like Mario Puzo's *Godfather*, with his gorillas around him. I kept quiet for a moment before finally answering him.

'I'm driven by a force that makes me want to know the *truth*, Mister Anzules! Something that I assume you are mostly good at hiding!'

'The *truth*?' asked Anzules, before violently hitting his desk with both hands. 'Well, tell me, what is the *truth*?'

He stood up. He moved away from his desk and opened a door to let someone into the room.

'This is Sergio, who I am sure you have had the opportunity to meet before,' explained Anzules, while Sergio took his place among the other monsters. 'Sergio is one of my very best employees; he has been working for me for as long as I can remember. We were at school together. When I founded my very first company, he was there to help me. At every stage of my life, Sergio has been there for me.'

Sergio looked quite pleased with the praise.

'This is a man, you see, who knows what the *truth* is,' added Anzules, walking around the room. 'Sergio infiltrated the *Aztlān Project* organisation on my behalf, about ten years ago. He has acted all along as *"Simple-minded Sergio"*. Ten years with the same act! He easily deserves an Oscar, because they never found out who he really was! Ten very long years gathering information about the Aztlāns, their activities, their members, their plans… All the information that I needed to get my *Aztlān Project* started.'

Anzules came close to me. He kneeled in front of me.

'You see, Sergio really knows everything about me and my activities. He might actually even know me better than I know myself!'

Anzules then took a big golden gun out of his jacket and pointed the weapon at my right temple.

'And still…'

Anzules suddenly turned to Sergio, aimed and shot him in cold blood, with five bullets in the head.

'… he knew far too much!'

I was shocked. For a moment, I really thought that he was going to shoot me. But nobody else seemed to be shocked by what had just happened. Even the music didn't stop. Without any particular expression on their faces, three of the gorillas immediately removed Sergio's body before coming back into the room.

'I just couldn't keep someone like him in my organisation any longer,' the rich man finished, standing up, 'since I must now clean my doorstep… because of you!'

He sat back at his desk, where piles of documents and a laptop were hiding a large glass of red wine he had just been served by a gorgeous blond in a very short red dress, who left just as quickly as she entered the room.

'So, thanks to my wife, you know who I am, you know what I do, and you know what I want to do! Is that not a marvellous coincidence? Because, you see, I also know who you are, I know what you do, and I know what you want to do! So, I would like to make a last effort to try to smooth the edges with you! I've just had a position freed so there's a vacancy with an unbeatable salary and very competitive benefits, and you surely have the skills for the job with your spirit, your expertise, your ethics… What do you think? Would you like to work with me? Would you like to work for me?'

'You must be joking!' I answered immediately, with disgust. 'Never in a million years would I work for you! There are things in life that are intrinsic. To me, one of them is to fight for justice and truth through my work. Unfortunately, I've learned that these two words are totally incompatible with you and your organisation. So, please, allow me to politely refuse your offer, Mister Anzules!'

The billionaire sat deep in his big black leather chair and sipped his wine, while staring me in the eyes. Then the music stopped downstairs. I could see the audience clapping and cheering the great Arturo O'Farrill saluting the crowd.

'I knew you would refuse my offer,' Anzules replied, 'but I still kept hope deep inside that you would maybe consider it… Do you like jazz, Mister Duprés?'

'I do! Particularly Arturo O'Farrill, who is one of the best jazzmen around…'

'Well, you see, life can be jazzy sometimes. Let me tell you something that you won't be around to witness: my plan will be successful! Listen, my virus will spread all over the world for days and weeks. People will be scared, governments too. The media will spread the fear all over the world. Then once the virus has spread enough, my men at the World Health Organization will *lobby* to step up the threat level of the virus and call it a pandemic. In the meantime, Sanniflu will have already been sold to millions and *Borgia Labs* will have made a huge profit too. Finally, the

WHO will ask all major laboratories to produce a vaccine, and all the countries on this planet will fight against time to guarantee their people that they will be able to protect them. They'll pay a lot of money for a vaccine. Because they will think they need one. And money will flow, money will flow… My companies will make a lot of money, and I will make a real fortune out of a bogus influenza virus!'

'What do you mean by *"bogus"*?' I asked, quite intrigued.

96. Breaking News.

The Health of the World, UK.

The World Health Organization (WHO) decided on Wednesday to raise the current level of influenza pandemic alert from phase 4 to phase 5, "based on assessment of all available information, and following several expert consultations." The sudden change of level of alert is to be seen as a big signal to all governments, the pharmaceutical industry, and the business community that specific actions must now be "undertaken with increased urgency and at an accelerated pace." WHO also said they want to track the pandemic at the epidemiological, clinical, and virological levels. "We do not have all the answers right now, but we will get them," concluded the WHO Director-General.

97. When it all makes sense…

7.56 p.m.

Anzules was all smiles. He finished his glass of wine before explaining himself.

'You see, I have done everything to make sure that if the authorities were to try to find out who was behind the outbreak of the virus, neither my companies nor myself would ever need to worry. One example of that is that little boy called *Patient zero*, in Cholula. One of your biggest mistake was to actually follow the clues that Sergio had sowed around you, such as suggesting you to go and visit the little boy's parents. I know that you spent some time there, met his parents, and that you sent a sample of his hair to London to get it analysed. The only thing that this analysis will prove is that the only people who die from the virus are Tlaxcalans descendants.'

'Which will help incriminate the Aztlāns...'

'Exactly! You see, before your visit to Cholula, Sergio had spoken to a young man who you later met and who introduced you to the little boy's parents. Sergio asked him to let you take a sample of his hair, so that you would prove the Aztlāns were innocent of the outbreak. It was actually the complete opposite and you fell into our trap. But now let me tell you something about the H1N1 virus. It is not the threat to humanity that the media and politics love to talk about daily, everywhere in the world. Not at all. You see, it's a simple flu virus genetically programmed to target a particular ethnic background. Of course, it could be used as a terrible weapon of mass extermination if used by the wrong people... if you see what I mean...'

He smiled. I didn't like that ugly smile. Then his behaviour changed again.

'As for the Aztlāns, don't forget that their bloody organisation is illegal and they also have some strong anti-Spanish manifestos! I have enough proof compiled against them over the years, thanks to the late Sergio, to get all their members arrested and put in jail for a very long time!'

It sounded like Anzules hated the Aztlāns more than anything, even more than the Cardinals, but I couldn't really understand his reason.

'What is it about the Aztlāns?' I asked, trying to find a way to free myself from the ropes I was bound to the chair with. 'I thought you hated the most powerful Cardinals of the Vatican, not the harmless *Aztlān Project…*'

'I hate both of them to be honest, but there's one thing that I have in common with the Aztlāns that makes me hate them even more than the Cardinals: they also want to recover the *Codex* that I have been trying to get for more than twenty years now, which is in the hands of the Vatican. They are a threat to my success. And I swear if there is a way for me to get rid of them, I'll do all that is in my power to make it happen!'

'So, tell me if I'm wrong… You started by using the virus to threaten the Vatican so that they would give you the *Codex?*'

Anzules nodded the head.

'But the virus was also intended to create a panic in the world,' I added, 'so that people would buy your laboratory's drugs en masse, which would have the amazing effect of making your subsidiaries get the highest profits ever seen in the pharmaceutical industry and, finally, make your company the only one in the world to achieve super profits during the current financial crisis.'

The rich man nodded again.

'And finally, you used the virus to kill Tlaxcalan descendants in Mexico and around the world, so that after analysing their DNA and comparing it with the virus' genetic composition, the authorities would be led to believe that there was in fact a criminal intention behind the outbreak of the virus. And as the good man that you are, you would provide the police with all the information that would, once and for all, show the *Aztlān Project* as a terrorist organisation, and the only people who could be blamed for the creation of such a virus simply because their Mexica ancestors were enemies of the Tlaxcalans.'

Anzules stood up suddenly with a huge smile on his face and clapped his hands. He turned to his gorillas and signalled for them to clap their hands too. I couldn't believe that I was given a round of applause by a gangster and his men.

'Bravo!' he shouted, still applauding. 'That's really impressive! I absolutely love it! That's why we had to catch you quick, otherwise you would be out there, spreading the news around the globe, and my plan would fail…'

'Why keep me alive then?'

'Well, you see, I wanted to share with you that great moment of joy when I declare myself the supreme winner and you the greatest loser of this story!'

Three of his men then came close to me. One of them, who was cross-eyed, forced me to open my mouth and he put a small grenade inside. At the sight of the grenade in front of me, and then the feel of it inside my mouth, I started panicking.

'What you are experiencing right now is quite uncomfortable, isn't it? Don't worry, it won't take long before this discomfort disappears, believe me! Ha, ha, ha… I'm ever so glad to have had a chance to meet you, Mister Duprés! I must go now, but be assured that I will be thinking of you later when eating at my favourite restaurant in town, the *Spotted Pig*!'

98. Breaking News.

BTVB News, UK.

In a TV address, Mexican President Felipe Calderon has announced the suspension of non-essential work and services from 1 to 5 May. Schools are already closed, public gatherings restricted, and archaeological sites placed off-limits. President Calderon also urged all Mexicans to stay in, saying there was, "No place as safe as your own home." He assured them that Mexico was well-stocked with anti-viral medicines and urged them against jumping to conclusions, suggesting the possibility that the virus originated outside Mexico.

In the meantime, health experts were focusing on the surroundings of a pig farm located in Santa Isabel Cholula, near the city of Puebla.

99. New York.

8.02 p.m.

The Spotted Pig? At that moment, I knew I was in New York! I admit that it took me an incredibly long time to understand that I was in the *Big Apple*, but when Anzules pronounced the name of that restaurant, my brain just declared, *"Eureka!"* I knew that gastro-pub pretty well since it was there that I first met my fiancée Sarah while she was a waitress there to finance her gap year in the US.

Anzules left the room with four of his men. The other two stayed, just staring at me. I knew the grenade in my mouth wasn't live, but it still had the powerful effect of scaring me.

But I decided that I wasn't going to be deterred by that; instead I was going to try my very best to unbind my hands from the rope. To do so, I was going to use my new black *Alessi* watch, which was a bit of a James Bond watch in fact. It projected the time onto my wrist using a modulated laser scanner with a laser beam that could cut one's skin off if too highly-powered. The watch looked like a fancy offset wrist bracelet and was still only a concept watch when a good friend at Alessi gave it to me for Christmas.

Even though both my hands were tied up behind my back, I put my right hand in such a position that would allow the miniature laser diodes to come to life so the laser of the watch would be released on the rope and burn it. The longer I pressed the *Alessi* button on top of the watch, the stronger the laser would become. I pressed the button and immediately started feeling the heat of the laser on the surface of my wrist. I directed the watch with my left hand so that the laser burnt through the rope rather than my skin.

After a few seconds, there was a slight smell of burning around me. But the two guards weren't paying enough attention to have spotted it. They were now both sitting on wooden chairs, right behind Anzules' desk, reading some comic strips.

As I felt the binding getting looser, I stopped the laser and then tried tearing the rope by moving it apart. A last effort and it worked! Both hands were now free behind me and the rope was getting so loose that it started falling off the floor.

That's when I stood up from the chair, removed the grenade from my mouth and held it out to the two men, who had been far too slow to react.

'If you two guys try anything to stop me, I will have to throw the live grenade to you!' I threatened them. 'Is that well understood?'

They nodded their heads. I asked them to slide their guns on the floor towards me, then ordered one of them to bind his friend to his chair. Once I was armed with their weapons, I left the grenade on the desk and tied up the other gorilla to his chair.

I was free to go. However, I wondered what had happened to Alicia. Had they taken her to New York too, or was she still in Mexico?

'Where is Alicia?' I asked one of the two men in black. 'Where is Anzules' wife? Is she here? Is she in New York?'

'I don't know, sir,' he answered, before starting to cry like a baby, along with his colleague.

I felt pity for these guys who looked so tough on the outside, but were totally scared and weak on the inside. As I wasn't going to get any answers from them, I needed to find Alicia by myself. I tore up two pieces of cloth that I found on the white sofa by the door, and muzzled the two men with them.

On Anzules' desk, I found my passport, my iPhone, and my wallet, which they had left in a transparent plastic bag on top of a pile of documents. The little blue book had disappeared though. I tried to open the small cupboards to find it, but everything was locked. I decided to give up on the book. Then I slowly opened the door and carefully made my way along the dark corridor.

The door closed behind me; I was in the complete dark, but I could still hear a piano being played in the club. I thought that if I followed the music, I would find some light and find my way out.

I found the stairs and had gone down three or four steps, when I heard a woman's voice. I went back upstairs and after following the wall for a while, I found a door. Through the keyhole, I could only see Alicia sitting on a blue sofa; she was suddenly twice slapped in the face by Anzules, before he and his gorillas took her to another room.

I tried to open the door without success. It was definitely locked from the inside. I went back to the stairs and slowly made my way towards the music. There was a door and some light there. I opened the door and behind it, there was the stage of the jazz club with a man playing the piano on one side, and seats and tables on the other. There was also a bar with all kind of bottles and drinks behind the two bartenders. The club was already half-empty as many people were leaving. Discreetly making my way towards the exit amongst the crowd, I noticed a large poster in the main hall with a picture of my jazz idol:

Muppets Jazz Bar

Arturo O'Farrill Solo

Playing Tonight: 7:00 pm – 8:00 pm / Price: $10

Once in the street, the temperature difference between here and Mexico was obvious. My t-shirt wasn't enough for New York. It was already evening. When I looked at my watch, I realised that I had lost a complete day between when I was at the institute with Alicia and my unexpected meeting with Anzules.

I didn't know what the rich man had planned for Alicia and where she was going to be taken exactly. But I knew the moment someone entered the room where I had tied up my two guards, the alert would be given to everyone in Anzules' gang. I had to leave right now and leave Alicia behind.

I quickly hailed a taxi. Surprisingly for a city like New York where it's always quite difficult to get one, a yellow cab stopped in front of me a few seconds later. A fifty-year-old Latino opened his window.

'Where d'you wanna go, dude?' he asked in a strong accent.

I was quickly checking my emails on my iPhone to know whether Alicia's friend at the institute in Mexico had followed her guidelines and sent an email to me. The taxi driver screamed at me again.

'Hey, dude! You getting in or not?'

I hadn't received anything. I jumped into the car. The driver was staring at me, a blue beret on the head and a cigarette in one hand.

'Where d'you wanna go?' he repeated with a fake smile, displaying the chewing gum in his mouth.

Why had she not contacted me yet? I had to get back to Mexico as soon as possible to find Alicia's friend at the institute, and find the documents.

'Take me to JFK Airport, please!' I answered.

100. Manuel.

8.39 p.m.

I was only in his car for two minutes on my way to the airport and the driver was already telling me the story of his life. Manuel had been married and divorced nine times, had sixteen children from six different mothers, and twenty-nine step-children. He also told me that he had worked as a butcher when he arrived in this country, he loved New York, he loved America, his dream was to drive a Formula Indy car, and many other *"God bless America"* statements, bla-bla-bla…

'And where you going? London? Paris? Rome?' he asked me.

'Mexico.'

'Mexico? Dude, I coming from Mexico!' he announced with real joy this time. 'You needing help find hotel or restaurant there?'

'That's fine thanks, I'm going there for business and I already have a hotel there. But thanks anyway…'

'All right, all right.'

Silence, finally. But not for long.

'What business you gonna do in Mexico?'

'I'm a journalist and I'm investigating there…' I answered simply, trying to avoid any further questioning.

But my answer didn't put him off. And he kept on asking questions after questions. I finally came out and told him I was going to meet someone at the *Institute of Anthropological Research.*

'Dude, it's really small world, one of my nephews working there! His name Orlando, and he know everybody there!'

'Are you kidding?'

'Dude, I no joking with my country!' Manuel assured me, extremely seriously, before smiling and coming back to our conversation. 'I calling him and I asking him meet you at airport in Mexico City… if you like? It's no problem to me. No problem. I can help. I can calling him. Right now. I call?'

I accepted. If my driver's nephew really did know everyone at the institute, I certainly had a chance of finding Alicia's friend there. Browsing the Internet on my iPhone, I managed to find a direct flight to Mexico City, with *Mexicana,* at about one o'clock in the morning. It was the earliest flight available and I would be in Mexico at five o'clock. I immediately booked my ticket online and received confirmation by email.

As we got to a traffic light, Manuel grabbed his red Nokia mobile phone from the passenger's seat, quickly dialled a number, and started speaking in Spanish. I showed Manuel the details of my flight on my iPhone. We moved again before reaching some more traffic lights. Five minutes later, Manuel turned to me and proudly told me his nephew was going to be waiting for me with a sign at the arrivals hall of the airport.

After almost an hour on the road, we eventually made it to JFK Airport. The famous terminal was fully illuminated and one could see plane after plane flying just above our heads.

'Thanks for the ride!' I told Manuel, paying him with my credit card, obviously having no American dollars with me. 'I was lucky to have found you, Manuel. I hope your nephew will be able to help me in Mexico.'

I was outside the car speaking to Manuel while many other taxis started queuing behind us.

'No problem, dude!' he replied, before carelessly waving at me and quickly leaving for another client, a beautiful young woman who was calling him from a distance.

Manuel really was a funny little man.

101. Breaking News.

Shares Watcher, USA.
The dumbest investment of the week.

Is the Swine Flu a wonderful investment opportunity, or is it not? Well, it all depends on the long-term factor. If the laboratories manage their marketing well and get their vaccines and other drugs to generate some good sales, one or maybe more companies could definitely become a winner. "This really is a short-term event we are talking about," said a spokeswoman for the stock analysis newsletter 'The Red Broker Investments'. "Will these companies make big profits out of a simple flu? No way. Unless the Swine Flu turns out to be a miracle for those currently running out of money."

One would certainly need to create some new products to attract people's interest, and also have a good marketing team to be able to sell the Swine Flu around the world. "If the Swine Flu is taken out of the equation, there is no reason left to trade in these companies at all." The selling figures of some of these companies will surely double, triple, or even quadruple, since we are in the middle of a crisis.

But honestly, investing in these laboratories would be like throwing bank notes out the window!

"Kill a man, and you are a murderer.
Kill millions of men, and you are a conqueror.
Kill everyone, and you are a god."
– Jean Rostand (1894 – 1977)

CHAPTER 11. TIME TO DIE

Die [verb] – to cease being a living creature.

(Excerpt from the Storyteller Dictionary)

102. Meeting Claudia.

Day 6 – 30th April 2009, 5.43 a.m.

When I got to Mexico's airport early Thursday morning, I met with Manuel's nephew, Orlando, who was an English speaker, thankfully! We quickly got on well. He told me that he had been working at the institute for nearly two decades and claimed to really know everyone on the campus. Before driving me to the institute, the thirty-eight-year old confirmed that he did have a colleague called Claudia and that she was actually working through the night.

Orlando called her directly in her office. She answered that she was too busy at first; she was even about to refuse to meet me until he said my name. Then she changed her mind and asked him to bring me to the institute as soon as possible. The man drove me all the way there, where I would eventually meet her forty minutes later, at the very same car park I had been abducted from two days earlier.

Orlando's car stopped in front of the main entrance of the building. An old woman was standing behind the glass door with long white curly hair, a white uniform, and a mobile phone in her hand. It was still very early in the morning. The sun was rising on the horizon.

As we passed the door, Orlando quickly introduced me to Claudia, but she wasn't very interested. She looked very agitated and anxious. She simply asked Orlando to leave us.

'I know who you are, Mister Duprés,' she announced, immediately taking me to a small corridor where we went through door after door. 'Did they follow you?'

'They? Right, you mean *they*? No, I don't think so. Well, I didn't see them anywhere since we left the airport.'

'Where is she? She hasn't contacted me, neither has she answered my messages! Where is she?'

After explaining what had happened when Alicia and I were last at the institute, Claudia opened the door to her office. The large room was absolutely chaotic with books, documents, newspapers cuttings, and other sheets literally covering the floor. She asked me to take a seat on one of the extremely uncomfortable green plastic chairs, while she climbed on her chair to start looking for the documents she knew I had come for, somewhere in a cupboard on top of the huge library behind her desk.

'Alicia asked me to keep these documents in case something happened to her,' she explained. 'I don't actually know much about her research. But I know that she got involved with something bigger than she imagined and when she felt things were turning bad, she told me about you and your quest.'

'My quest?' I asked, surprised.

'Your quest for the truth to be unveiled, as she put it. She told me that you were trustworthy and that you only deserved these documents because she knew you would put them to good use.'

She found them. As she came down from the chair, she handed me a blue folder that she said contained the documents. I suddenly heard a very loud sound coming from the window. Claudia immediately fell heavily on the floor, just as if she had fainted. But I realised she had been shot in the back when I saw three stains of blood on the back of her white uniform.

Then I heard two other shots passing through the window again. I jumped to the floor and hid behind her desk. Claudia's body was there, by my side, lifeless. There was no pulse. I couldn't be surer that Anzules' gang was behind her assassination. But she was certainly not the main target. How could they have known she was in possession of the documents? They surely didn't know that. Unless Alicia had told them so. But would she have talked?

No, it was obvious to me they had tried to kill me one more time and failed yet again. But this time, I could be sure of one thing: they were not going to let me get out of the institute alive. I tried to have a discreet look at the window to see where the shots were coming from, when I heard four other shots and quickly hid under the desk again.

What could I do to escape these guys? Would I be able to get Orlando to help me? With the big blue folder in my hands, I quickly made my way to the door without being seen or shot. I opened the door, stood up, and started running down the corridors. I found Orlando at the reception, talking to two bald men dressed in black. I immediately stopped and entered the closest room. It was a small dark classroom. I was watching the discussion through a window. Now that they had sneaked into the building, any mistake could be fatal to me.

I knew that Orlando didn't have a clue what was going on and didn't know anything about Alicia's documents. I couldn't hear anything, but the men in black clearly didn't believe him. They put him face to the ground within seconds, pointing their guns at him.

Only one of them was holding him there while the other went off looking for me in the corridor. Orlando had obviously told them where I was meeting Claudia. I had to eliminate these two men in order to be able to speak to Orlando. I made a loud noise using chalk on the blackboard in my classroom, so it would attract their attention to me.

It worked. The man in the corridor came close to the classroom to have a look. He first looked inside, through a window. Then he slowly opened the door and eventually entered the room. I was hiding inside a wooden closet where many books and a human skeleton with a tag saying *"Señor Mendes"* were kept away from the dust. I temporarily borrowed *Mister Mendes'* place while he was outside, smiling at the man in black.

When the man closed his door, I silently slid mine open and jumped on him in the middle of the classroom as he was about to move towards the first rank of students' desks. We both fell on the floor. I stood up as quickly as I could and kicked him hard in the stomach. His gun escaped from his hand, sliding across the floor, but I managed to grab it quite easily.

I immediately pointed the weapon in his direction and instructed him not to speak by putting my forefinger on my mouth. I didn't want him to raise the alarm by shouting anything to his companions. The poor man was moaning in pain after the kick I had given him. With the gun in my hand, I asked him to stand up. But as he violently grabbed my foot to trip me up, I accidentally fired the gun and shot him twice in the head.

Silence. The gun was equipped with a suppressor, so there would hardly have been any noise coming from the room. The man fell heavily onto the floor. I checked his pulse, he was dead.

103. Breaking News.

TRZ Today, USA.

New Yorkers have survived transit strikes, bankruptcy, financial crisis, blackouts, and terrorist attacks. So

to many, the Swine Flu is regarded with a fatalistic
and bewildered calm as just another calamity. "When you
live in New York, you don't have much of a choice,"
explains Hillary, a 62-year-old housewife, planning for
a vacation in Guatemala. "You must adapt to every
situation in this city and think that whatever has to
happen, it will happen! Then life goes on anyway!"

104. The way down.

7.02 a.m.

I had been through a few tough investigations before, but I had
never had to kill anyone. What had to happen happened: I had just killed a
man because of the Swine Flu virus.

I couldn't just stand there, staring at his still body lying on the
floor, I had to do something, and quick. I hid the body upright in the
wooden closet. Then I gave a little clean to the floor with a jumper a
student had probably forgotten in the classroom, trying to erase any trace
of blood. Finally, I had another look at the reception where Orlando was
still being held on the floor at gunpoint.

I opened the door of the classroom. The bald man at the reception
wasn't particularly watchful, so I managed to approach him quite easily
and as he was about to turn around, I pointed my gun in his lower back.
We stayed there for about a minute without a word. Then he turned around
and looked at me, totally gutted. His eyes were more upset than he would
show.

The strong man removed his foot from Orlando's back, and I hit
his head with the butt of my gun. I helped Manuel's nephew stand up and
asked him to find us a place to dispose of the man. He looked at me for a
moment and we took the body to the cleaners' room. I borrowed the man's
gun and presented it to Orlando.

'Who are you?' he asked me, locking the room from the outside. 'Who are these men?'

'It's a long story…' I answered, while going to get the blue folder I had left in the classroom.

I returned to him.

'To put everything in a nutshell, I'm a journalist and I've been investigating the Swine Flu virus for the last five days. During that short period of time, I've discovered some very important things about the virus and who is really behind the outbreak.'

'And these people want to kill you now?'

'That's right!'

'Why did you want to come to the institute in the first place?' Orlando asked, somewhat dubious. 'Why did you want to meet Claudia?'

'I had to come here because Claudia was in possession of some important documents that prove everything I know about the conspiracy. Basically, this folder contains all the truth about the virus. I mustn't lose this folder; otherwise no one will ever know what the Swine Flu is all about!'

Orlando understood what I meant and was really keen on helping me quickly get out of the building and the campus. Even though I had only known him for an hour or two, the Mexican impressed me with his ability to act under pressure. He showed me a way of getting to an underground car park that he claimed only the teachers knew about.

We took a lift to go down to the basement. I hid my gun under my t-shirt behind my back. While in the lift, I opened the blue folder to have a glimpse at some of the documents Alicia had collected from Anzules' offices. I was absolutely baffled when I saw the signatures of some of the most important experts from the World Health Organization at the bottom of a page entitled:

Top Confidential Experts Agreement

with Anzules Group

Regarding H1N1 Virus 2010

– DO NOT DISCLOSE / SENSITIVE INFORMATION –

105. The Agreement.

Top Confidential Experts Agreement with Anzules Group
Regarding H1N1 Virus 2010, 22/06/2008.

The H1N1 influenza outbreak will begin in February 2010
in a farm located in Santa Isabel Cholula. It will then
quickly spread to Mexico City and other localities in
Mexico.

The undersigned twenty-five experts guarantee to
Anzules Group that they will lobby for the World Health
Organization and public health authorities to purposely
exaggerate the risks of the virus, and to create alarm
among the population of the world by declaring it a
pandemic.

The undersigned experts understand that the WHO will be
criticised by the media for its pandemic alert and its
handling of the situation pre- and post-pandemic. In no
circumstances shall Anzules Group be involved in the
matter, or involved in reports of conflicts of
interests between health officials and experts and
vaccine makers.

The undersigned experts agree that it is important that
the declaration of full pandemic isn't over until
Anzules Group finishes the production of the H1N1
vaccine, so that it can be sold to all countries in the
world at any time.

The undersigned experts also agree that if an assessment post-pandemic takes place by the United Nations agency's emergency committee, in no circumstances shall the name of Anzules Group or any of its subsidies be made public.

Any review should be conducted by some of the undersigned experts. Their preliminary findings shall be reported to Anzules Group first, with the final report to be published after 2011.

106. Orlando.

7.21 a.m.

'That's way too far!' I said out loud.

Orlando looked at me, unsure what I was talking about. 'Are you all right? You look a bit pale.'

'I… I'm all right, thanks. I… I just need to leave this place as quickly as possible!'

When the doors of the lift opened in front of us, I noticed that the car park was already fully illuminated. Orlando was the first out with his gun in his hand. I very suddenly had a strange feeling and decided to remain in the lift. I grabbed my gun and waited there.

Orlando reappeared a few seconds later, asking me why I was still in the lift. I didn't answer. As I looked him right in the eyes, I understood it all.

'You are one of them!' I noted, as the door was about to start closing. 'And all that happened at the reception was only a masquerade, wasn't it?'

Everything came to my mind. Anzules had planned it all. My kidnapping, my easy escape from the jazz club in New York, the Mexican taxi driver whose nephew was coincidentally working at the institute, the way out by the lift… It had all been far too easy to be true.

'What are you talking about?' Orlando asked, faking it very badly. 'Come on, follow me!'

'You know what I'm talking about, Orlando!'

The door was closing, but Orlando put his arm in front of the sensors and it reopened slowly.

'Right. I see that we can't hide anything from you, Mister Duprés, so I will tell you the truth. Mister Anzules has already chased and stopped his wife once in the past. He obviously knew she was plotting something against him. But even though he tortured her, she never spoke of or admitted to having stolen these documents in his office. As Mister Anzules really wanted to know where the documents were hidden, and his wife wasn't willing to speak, he decided to let her go so that, by following her, he would find them.

'That's when you had your first contact with her at the Basilicas. That's also when you first appeared on our radar. We have been following your every move ever since, all the way through the market and then to the institute. We even knew about your presence in Tlaxcala and Cholula. We have played tricks on you throughout your investigation. We dictated every decision you took so that in the end, you would lead us to the precious documents… And here they are, as expected, in your hands!'

'So you never really wanted to kill me at all, did you?' I asked.

'We wanted to scare you, not kill you. You were far too important to us. The whole thing was like a big cinema production. We had to make you believe you were in control all along. And you believed it!'

'What's next, then? Will you take the documents back to Anzules and simply kill me? I'm sure you don't need me any longer!'

'Spot on!'

Four bald men suddenly entered the lift as Orlando moved away. I didn't have time to fire on them before they disarmed me, taking the folder out of my hands and dragging me out of the lift. I couldn't fight but I tried anyway. These guys were so large and tall that whatever punch I gave, it seemed like they simply couldn't feel any pain at all.

I could, however, feel the pain as they repeatedly punched me one after the other, as well as kicking me in the back, in the stomach, in the face, my arms, literally everywhere. I was bleeding like I didn't know someone could ever bleed. I could even see my blood streaming down the floor of the car park. The beating was continuous. Endless. My eyes were burning, my nose broken. I couldn't speak anymore. I couldn't hear anything. The four men were certainly enjoying it. Orlando too. Maybe they were even avenging their colleague that I had shot in the classroom?

I was as weak as could be. I was reduced to the state of a punching ball. After maybe ten minutes of assault, my face was certainly completely deformed, I had probably three or four broken ribs, my clothes were full of blood, and my luck had definitely run out. My body was hurting so much, but the attack was still far from finished.

At one moment, I had a terrible thought. I wanted all this to end. I just wanted all this to end so badly, quick and sudden. For one moment, I forgot everything that mattered so much in my life. For one moment, I just forgot everything and everyone. For one moment, I became utterly selfish.

For one moment, I just wanted to die!

107. Breaking News.

Underestimated Press, USA.
Swine Flu: Advice for Schools.

President Obama has repeated on Wednesday how important it is to follow the hygiene guidance from the Centers for Disease Control (CDC). He also said that whenever a student or a group of students have a confirmed or suspected case of Swine Flu, their school should close temporarily.

*"The first step in a person's salvation
is knowledge of their sin."*
– Lucius Annaeus Seneca (c. 4 BC – AD 65)

CHAPTER 12. SALVATION

Salvation [noun] – the act of preserving or delivering someone from something harmful, the redemption from evil.

(Excerpt from the Storyteller Dictionary)

108. Angel or Demon?

7.45 a.m.

Orlando was about to leave me with his men, taking away the folder with the documents, when he came close to me to have a last word.

'I wish you a very good time with them, Mister Duprés!' he announced before making his way towards what I imagined was a door somewhere in the dark. 'They have been specially trained to deal with nosy people like you!'

As Orlando left, all of a sudden, a fifth man showed up.

'Can I play with you too?' he asked his colleagues.

The others spread away from me to leave some space for my next tormentor. I couldn't really see him, rather just guess about his figure. I understood the pain wasn't over yet.

I heard a gun being armed. What was he going to do? Was he going to shoot me? Was that what he meant by *playing*?

Then he fired four times…

When I opened my eyes, I still couldn't really see anything, but I thought that I was probably dead. I was still lying on the floor in a pool of blood, when a shadow came over to see me. Was it an angel or maybe a demon? Whoever it was, the shadow started speaking to me.

'How are you feeling?'

'Am I dead?' I asked, still in terrible pain. 'It hurts badly everywhere. I thought that one doesn't feel any pain at all after death…'

'That might be because you're not really dead!' the voice replied.

I tried to open my eyes as wide as possible only to see I was actually speaking to one of Anzules' men in black.

'My name is Miguel, and before you start freaking out, I must tell you that I'm an Aztlān…'

'You? An Aztlān?'

'Yes!'

My eyes started to visualise his face little by little, but everything was still quite blurry.

'Impossible.'

'I am!'

'Why is it that you look like Anzules' men in black, then?'

Opening my mouth to speak was very painful. I had been beaten up without mercy, and I couldn't feel anything but pain. Every muscle, every nerve, every bone in my body was aching.

'Before I explain, let me help you.'

Miguel helped me to slowly stand up. Every move was a struggle and I wasn't able to stand alone. I was staggering. Putting my left arm around his neck, he helped me to get to a big black car that belonged to the men in black. I started recovering my sight and could finally see my rescuer's face. Miguel was bald like every other gorilla of the gang, and he had an enormous scar from his right eye down to his mouth. He looked quite friendly, but I was keeping in mind Manuel and Orlando's fake friendliness. Once bitten, twice shy!

On the floor, not far from where the car was parked, I noticed the four bodies of the men who had taken pleasure in beating me up.

As he opened the door and helped me sit inside, I really felt like I had become the weakest man on the planet. My legs were heavy, my arms were bleeding, and most of my body wasn't responsive.

'Now let me explain… In 2008, I along with another member of our organisation, infiltrated what Anzules calls the *"Point Zero Team"* and what people call *"men in black"*. The Aztlāns knew that Anzules was planning something against them for quite some time, so I volunteered to infiltrate his people and live a life of gangster until we knew what the threat was all about.

'When Anzules got married, I met his wife, Alicia, who happened to be Carlos' youngest sister. Contrary to her brother, she wasn't an Aztlān, but she quickly discovered pretty much everything her husband was going to do with the Swine Flu virus. We became friends and she started trusting me. She gave us much information about how Anzules worked and what he was planning to do, but then she got caught stealing some documents about the virus. Anzules tortured her personally, but she didn't give away my cover and pretended that she was working on her own initiative. Alicia is a strong young woman!

'I was later told by our other infiltrated agent that Anzules had purposely let her escape,' Miguel continued, once at the wheel of the car, 'so he could find out where she had hidden the stolen confidential documents. Then you got involved and you met Carlos… Our organisation immediately asked me to keep an eye on you since the Aztlāns first thought you could be a threat because of your incorrect theories about us. But as your position started to change, their opinion about you changed too, and they realised that you were going to be in great danger if you were to ever get Alicia's documents in your hands.'

Miguel started driving around the underground car park to get to the exit.

'As they kidnapped you and Alicia, the *Point Zero Team* killed Carlos, after having tortured him too. This morning, the police found his body cut into pieces, in a place called *Jardines del Pedregal,* where the Mexicas used to send people who they had banished from the community, so they would be bitten by rattlesnakes living there.'

'I worked with Carlos a few years ago…'

'I know, Carlos told me.'

Miguel managed to get us out of the car park quite quickly, but someone was waiting for us outside. Eight gorillas armed with guns were standing by the entrance of the institute with three cars used as barricades. It looked like we were now going to be barred from leaving the institute.

But the *Point Zero Team* wasn't actually waiting for us. They were merely keeping the area under surveillance. Miguel asked me to bend down to hide from them.

Our vehicle slowly approached the barricades. Miguel flashed his lights four times to ask his colleagues to let him proceed through the gates of the institute. The three cars instantly moved away and our vehicle was allowed through without any problem.

I painfully sat back in my seat. As we joined the main road, Miguel accelerated to put distance between our enemies, as they would soon realise that four of them had been killed and Miguel himself had something to do with my escape.

109. Hidden.

8.18 a.m.

'As they killed Carlos, I had no choice but to get involved because your life was in danger,' Miguel continued, as we were getting to a familiar place, *Plaza de las Tres Culturas*, where I had previously met the priest from the *Aztlān Project*.

'I couldn't let them kill you since you're our only hope; the only person who knows the truth and who can prevent Anzules from destroying us and put him in jail…'

Miguel parked the car in a small street at the back of the *Templo de Santiago*. He helped me get out of the car and took me to the church. I was still walking with a limp, but I made it to the closed wooden door. Miguel knocked in some sort of sequence. The code was correct and the door opened with a loud creak.

There, two tall men dressed in black cassocks without clerical collars appeared. Miguel spoke to them in Spanish, asking them to help me while he was going to get rid of the car. He then told me that I was in a safe place now.

'Listen… you will meet someone very important in a minute, but these two men will look after you and your injuries first,' he told me, before leaving me in their hands.

We entered the church that was as cold as it was during my last visit. The two men dressed like priests took me to a broken statue of Saint James that I had noticed last time. One of them pressed the two hands of the sculpture for two or three seconds, and a hidden room suddenly appeared behind Saint James. It wasn't actually a room; it was a secret passage, a corridor leading to secret rooms.

One of these rooms without windows looked a bit like a place of surgery or a dentist's office, with a lot of medical tools on the desks and medical posters on the walls. Here, they helped me sit on a big chair before cleaning up my blood, stitching my cuts, and dealing with all my other injuries. They also gave me some painkillers, which I was grateful for.

The two priest-like men nursed me there for about twenty minutes in total silence. Several stitches, bandages, and some strong painkillers later, I was starting to feel better. Of course, I could still feel the pain everywhere in my body, but it was nonetheless much less of a struggle to move around. I had also recovered most of my intellectual faculties.

They then took me to another corridor and we went downstairs to another room, even darker than the corridor, where there was an ornamental, tidy desk with some books and a few sheets on it. An interesting fact was that the sculptured decorations on the desk looked very similar to a picture I remembered from Alicia's little blue book, coming from the Codex Mendoza. The picture was representing Moctezuma II as the *Tlatoani of Tenochtitlan*, the ruler of the city of Mexico before the Spanish Conquest.

111. Archives.

Nicypedia: Moctezuma's revenge.

Any cases of traveller's diarrhoea contracted by tourists visiting Mexico is colloquially called Moctezuma's revenge. About 40% of foreign travellers in Mexico get disrupted by the infection. Most cases are very mild and get resolved in a few days without treatment. Severe or extended cases, however, may result in a severe medical risk and could prove fatal

if mismanaged. The supervision of a medical
professional is definitely advised.

112. The last Tlatoani.

8.47 a.m.

I was sitting in front of that desk, on a sack-back Windsor armchair. It was a bit like being called to the headmaster's office in secondary school. I was at least as anxious as a teenager would be; waiting to know what fate had in store for me.

All of a sudden, the door opened and a man in his seventies came in, also dressed as a priest. He had a short white beard and was wearing a very thin pair of glasses.

'So, we meet again, Señor Duprés!' the man announced in a voice that sounded really familiar to me. 'Our last meeting had to be cut short because of some individuals who were chasing you. You must remember that. Don't worry, it won't happen this time, believe me!'

I eventually recognised the voice. He was the priest I had had a chat with in the confessional of this very church, just three days ago.

'I remember you, now. You're a senior member of the Aztlān Project, aren't you?'

The man smiled at me.

'I am sorry that I didn't have the time to introduce myself on our last encounter. Allow me to do so now… My name is Antonio Machado Moctezuma, but I am better known as Father Raúl in this community. I am the leader of the Aztlān Project organisation, I am its *Tlatoani*.'

'That explains these ornaments on your desk,' I replied, indicating the sculptures.

'These sculptures represent the last eleven rulers of the Mexica Empire,' the old man explained, showing them to me one after the other. 'From *Acamapichtli*, who was the first Mexica ruler, to *Cuauhtemoc*, the last before the fall of the Empire.'

He sat behind his desk.

'I have been leading my people for forty years now and it is the first time our organisation has been endangered by an individual as vile as Rodrigo Anzules.'

'Is this church your headquarters?' I asked, looking at the old paintings on the walls representing Mexicas in their daily life, as well as some battles and gods.

'It is indeed. But I am not a priest even though I dress like one and I am called *Father*. This is just a disguise to keep a very low profile in our society and to prevent the authorities from knowing who we really are and what we really do. For centuries, the Aztlāns have tried to act discreetly, looking for the right opportunities to make our voices heard, but ever since Anzules appeared, everything has changed, everything has become more dangerous to the thousands of us.'

'The man who brought me here told me he had successfully infiltrated Anzules' organisation and he had become friends with the billionaire's wife. If that's the case, why didn't you simply contact the authorities and warn them what Anzules was about to do with the virus?'

Moctezuma stood up, turned around, and grabbed a small black remote control. He pressed a button that switched off the lights in the room. The remote control was illuminated. He pressed another button and suddenly a projector started showing pictures on a screen in front of him.

The first of these pictures was one of Anzules, a cigar in his mouth, playing golf with Tiger Woods.

'You obviously already know this man, Rodrigo Stefano Borgia Anzules. He is one of the richest men in Latin America and the world. He is also very influential politically, especially in his own country, Guatemala, but also in Venezuela, Peru, Argentina, and in Mexico!'

Next on the screen, a map with each one of these countries highlighted, then the picture of the benches of the Mexican parliament.

'In this country alone, Anzules is said to count his supporters among three quarters of the politicians. That includes some ministers and their advisers, all corrupt.'

In the next picture, Anzules was in what seemed to be his traditional white suit, shaking hands with the President of Mexico, in front of small schoolchildren and journalists.

'He is also a very good friend of our president, as you can see! That man hasn't just built a business empire; he has literally built a protective bubble where you find celebrities, bankers, journalists, politicians, militaries, and even judges all together. He is therefore absolutely safe from anything or anybody. He is covered for anything he wants to do.'

'I understand. If you don't share the same fan club, it makes it very difficult to do anything against him.'

'Exactly! We cannot trust anyone within either the local or the federal governments. And I won't even mention the media!'

'Why did you approach me then?'

Next picture: Alicia.

'Through our two infiltrated agents, we had an ally within Anzules' organisation: his wife! Carlos' sister. She quickly told us that you were an external element, a foreign journalist investigating the virus. We kept an eye on you at first, but we soon understood you were our only hope. We tried to protect you against Anzules and his men several times. Some even sacrificed their lives for you to be here today, in front of me. Carlos, for example…'

I sighed.

'Now, you know the whole story and you know the truth. Because you are the chosen one!'

Next picture: me. Silence. This last sentence sounded far too theatrical to me. Though I didn't know what the old man was expecting from me at this stage, I was certainly going to be up for it.

'What should I do now?' I asked, feeling a challenge coming.

'You must return to Cholula and find anything, any clue that could prove that Anzules is behind the virus,' Moctezuma answered.

'What about Alicia?' I queried, as the Aztlān was switching the lights back on in the room.

'According to our two infiltrated agents, she has been transferred to another location somewhere in the United Kingdom. But we aren't yet sure where she is.'

'We must do something to free her from...'

'She is not our priority right now, Señor Duprés!' the old man interrupted me. 'We must concentrate all our efforts on finding proof against Anzules and his men to protect our organisation!'

'I can't believe you just said that! How come she's not a priority?' I asked, getting quite upset by his last comment. 'She has supplied your people with information that she stole from Anzules, putting her life at risk more than once... and you now suggest that we focus on something other than getting her free, for the sake of your secret organisation!'

'That's what we call sacrifice. Her brother did it and...'

'You cannot compare her to her brother, she isn't an Aztlān! And don't you start talking about sacrifice when the ones who are giving their lives aren't from your people! This has a totally different name to me: I call it recklessness!'

'We will deal with her situation after having secured some evidences against Anzules!' the old man replied calmly. 'Now that he is in possession of the documents, he will hurry to execute his evil plan and put the blame on us. Then the authorities will put us all under arrest and it will be the end of the *Aztlān Project*! Do you want to be responsible for wrecking thousands of lives because you tried to save one?'

I wanted to go and free Alicia, but I had to be more realistic considering thousands of people could be unfairly detained by the Mexican authorities for a crime they didn't commit.

'I want your word that after having found what you need against Anzules, you will help me free Alicia.'

'You have my word, Señor Duprés!' he answered, before we shook hands to seal the deal.

113. Archives.

RVOJ Mexico Bulletin, MEXICO. (August 1989)

Since early in the morning, foreign dignitaries have been arriving in Mexico to attend the state funeral of Antonio Machado Moctezuma, who died in a plane crash in Venezuela last Sunday. The urn with his ashes has been displayed to the public since his burnt remains were flown home on Wednesday.

The man who was considered by most as the father of modern Mexican archaeology was en route to a conference in Venezuela, last Friday, when his plane violently crashed in bad weather 12km west of Caracas. He was killed, along with his wife, his two assistants, and the plane's two pilots. The cause of the accident remains unknown.

Antonio Machado Moctezuma, 49, was a prominent Mexican archaeologist who excavated at the major archaeological sites in Mexico. Moctezuma changed the understanding of the Aztecs religion, empire, and ideology, through his lectures, writings, and museum exhibits. He received many honours and awards, both in Mexico and in other countries, for his passion for the Aztecs and his hard work.

Yesterday, President Carlos Salinas decreed today as a national day of mourning in tribute to Antonio Machado Moctezuma.

114. Some passion.

9.14 a.m.

'Now, Señor Duprés, you must return to Cholula and meet Patient zero again.'

'Why him?'

'Because the boy was probably the first person infected by the virus; he might hold the key that led to the outbreak. You need to check with his parents if he has ever been in or played near Anzules' farm. If it is the case, the little boy could help us prove that the farm is responsible for the outbreak.'

'We will certainly need more than that to nail Anzules!' I answered, doubtfully. 'Besides, Anzules also now has the little blue book in the hands, so he must know everything about Jaca as we speak! I'd rather go to Jaca quickly so that…'

'Stop it!' Moctezuma shouted, which silenced me pretty much immediately. 'You… you must now go to Cholula because that is your mission! That is what you are here for and that is why you have been sent to us!'

The old man, who looked quite nice and jovial at first, was in fact a rude and arrogant individual. He was behaving in a very unpleasant manner, and I started thinking he was acting as if I was one of the members of the *Aztlān Project*. Giving me orders. Telling me what to do.

'One of our English-speaking members, Father Michael, will take you there this morning,' Moctezuma added, as two other men, also dressed like priests, entered the room. 'You need to be there as soon as possible to gather fresh evidences. Father Michael, please take Señor Duprés to Cholula as planned.'

Father Michael, who was a tall black man with short hair, beckoned me to follow him. He would later tell me he was actually born in the United States, in the city of Page, in Arizona.

As we were leaving the room, the second priest was stroking his grey moustache and twirling his black and white glasses between his fingers while staring at me thoughtfully. When we were out of the room, I overheard the little priest talking to Moctezuma in English.

'Is he really the one?' he asked, sounding sceptical.

'I also doubted it at first, George, but remember what the Codex says: *Because he, who questioned the decisions of the last of the Tlatoanis, was the one who last sacrificed his life for the rebirth of a new Mexica Empire...*'

Sacrifice my life? What was that all about? It sounded like some kind of scripture or prophecy to me. I wasn't going to be reduced to doing what a religious book wanted me to do. I had no intention of risking my life just so the Aztlāns could recreate their lost Empire. I didn't mind dying for the truth, but certainly not for some nostalgic people.

I left the corridor and joined Father Michael in a car waiting for us in the backyard of the church. The difference of the temperature between the old building and the outside was like day and night. Passing through the door of the church, I felt like I was entering a sauna.

115. Excerpt from *"The Aztlān Codex"*.

CHAPTER 2.

"THE CURSE".

...and from the big house with boars, near the small blessed village, came the great calamity. It disseminated from soul to soul because of the Dark Soul's curse. When the calamity reached the big village, the earth trembled and the curse covered the surface of the world. But the curse didn't kill all the souls of the world, for the Dark Soul only wanted to scare the nine great shamans of the ancient world and show them the extent of his power.

Crossing the ocean, a beautiful soul from the ancient world brought the good news to the Aztlāns. He was known as the Eastern Eagle. He battled against the foolish creatures sent by the Dark Soul, but he survived all their efforts.

On another very hot day, the Eastern Eagle met the last of the Tlatoanis at the Temple, where they shared thoughts and ideas with much passion. The Eastern Eagle was then recognised as the Aztlāns' only salvation. Because he, who questioned the decisions of the last of the Tlatoanis, was the one who last sacrificed his life for the rebirth of a new Mexica Empire.

116. Vanished.

10.46 a.m.

We drove for an hour and a half to Santa Isabel Cholula. Almost at the entrance of the little town, I desperately tried to find the sign announcing the farm, *Granja Dodgson*, but it had vanished. Was it due to vandalism?

When we eventually found the small road leading to the farm, I noticed that the buildings seemed different from the ones I had previously seen. Was it actually the same farm? The landscape looked the same. The dirty roads had been completely replaced by macadamised ones. The heavily electrified gate, the CCTV system, the warning signs, and the tough guards with their electric prods had all gone. No tractor in the fields, no large silver buildings, no smell of swine.

We slowly approached the main entrance where the only two guards standing around had nothing to do with the ones I had met when I was here with Federico. They were dressed in a red and grey uniform, and they weren't carry any weapons.

'Are we in the right place?' asked Father Michael, a bit surprised by what he could see.

'I would have thought so, but this isn't the same farm…'

'Well, it's simply not a farm at all. There's a sign over there saying that this is actually an environment control agency belonging to the Department of Health!'

'Are you serious?'

'I am!'

There was even the seal of the Mexican ministry on the sign. Father Michael stopped the car in the middle of the empty road and we went together to ask the two guards a few questions.

They told the American priest that there had never been any farm in this location.

'They claim that they have been working here for the last three years and they have never heard of any big pig farm in the region,' Father Michael translated, as he moved away from the gates.

'It's impossible!' I shouted out loud. 'I came here just two days ago with a young man who I met in Cholula. We even managed to meet some senior staff in that very same building!'

I pointed at the big building I had visited that had now been painted green.

'They say that they can't let us in without a prior appointment. And according to them, it can take up two weeks to get one!' Father Michael told me.

Everything I saw on the farm had now vanished and been replaced by some big machines, big weather balloons, instruments to measure the wind, and some other equipment.

'It's just as if this place changed totally in the space of a few hours! I didn't dream it though! The farm was definitely here!'

Suddenly, the Aztlān urged me to get back into our car. He had noticed a black car coming towards us which he recognised as one of the *Point Zero Team*'s. We immediately drove away and made our way to Cholula instead, to go and visit Miguel Serez's parents again.

As we were entering the little town, I realised that something had also changed there: the road was paved! Then we entered Cholula where the streets were absolutely unrecognisable. When I first visited the town, the streets were a mix of mud and unfinished macadam, with maybe only a few metres of paved road. Now, it looked like all the works in Cholula had finally been completed. Within two days, it had miraculously become a properly paved town. I couldn't believe my eyes.

I directed Father Michael to the neighbourhood where the four-year-old boy lived and we finally stopped in front of their blue house. I was quite happy to see that the house hadn't vanished or changed as everything else had. But there weren't any children playing in the street. The town looked quite spooky without anyone in the streets. I realised that we hadn't seen anyone on the streets since we arrived.

The streets looked very clean and the houses looked quite good too. No more graffiti or cracks on the walls.

I led the way to Miguel's house and I rang the doorbell. Silence. I rang again. Still no one answered. I rang a third time. Finally, a woman came to open the door, but it wasn't Miguel's mother. The woman started shouting at us. Father Michael tried to calm her by explaining who we were and who we wanted to see, but she kept on shouting for another five minutes. As he tried to understand what was going on, she eventually angrily slammed the door on us.

'She said she didn't want you to ever come to ring at her door again,' Father Michael told me, heading back to the car. 'She first claimed that she didn't know who Miguel Serez was or where he lives, then she said that everyone in town has been warned you would probably come to see them one day. She said you are a dangerous evil soul seeking revenge on the people of Cholula, you have special powers, and you created the virus so everyone in town would get sick and die. Lastly, she said that you're back to get everybody who didn't die already.'

'Who told her such a foolish thing?'

'As far as I understand it, she said it was a rich man who came to town two days ago, to give a sermon and a blessing to everyone in the open air, before offering to make Cholula the brightest town in Mexico if all the residents refused to help you and avoid speaking to you the day you came here…'

'Well, that could explain the welcome banners and the crowd that we didn't see!' I joked. 'And who do you think that rich man was?'

'Anzules!' we stated together.

Once in the car, we drove back to the capital while trying to understand what had happened in Cholula.

'So, Anzules came to Cholula two days ago with his men, probably after your visit, and told everyone that they should avoid you because you were some sort of demon. I am not at all surprised that people listened to him because people in this country are very superstitious. Then he offered to redecorate their town, their streets, and their houses. Everything to make them happy. So he quite obviously became the good guy... and you the bad one!'

But two things were still missing: Miguel Serez and the farm.

'As his men transformed the town, they must have also transformed the farm with the precious help of some people he must have corrupted in the Mexican government. As for the two guards, they were certainly told not to say a word about the farm and to make us go away as quickly as possible, with the help of the *Point Zero Team* appearance!' Father Michael noted.

Father Michael was a clever man. I just couldn't say a word because I was thinking that he was certainly right.

'Miguel Serez's case is more complicated. I think they must have moved them away from Cholula to a secret location, somewhere close to a beach, say Cancun, or even abroad, with enough money not to worry about anything in life again. Then they must have offered the house to the woman we met, who has been brainwashed with Anzules' stories about demons, like everyone else in town!'

His analysis of the situation was so crystal clear that I had nothing to add to it.

117. Excerpt from *"The Aztlān Codex"*.

CHAPTER 3.

"THE DARK SOUL".

But a shadow was following us all: an evil soul that was known to the wise men as the Dark Soul. He was the nightmare in person. But he was also a demon with a beautiful smile, a smooth betrayer, a snake that could easily poison any innocent soul with his gentle words and his gentle manners. He was pure evil. Many innocent souls believed his speech for they were listening to what they wanted to hear. And as they became deaf, the poison wasn't poison to them anymore, it was simply honey. But the truth is it was nothing but a poison that was making its way all over their bodies and their minds.

*"The journey is difficult, immense.
We will travel as far as we can,
but we cannot in one lifetime
see all that we would like to see
or to learn all that we hunger to know."*
– Loren Eiseley (1907 – 1977)

CHAPTER 13. THE LAST JOURNEY

Journey [noun] – an act of travelling from one place to another.

(Excerpt from the Storyteller Dictionary)

118. Not a bad idea.

1.22 p.m.

'So, what are we going to do now that we have absolutely nothing left to incriminate Anzules?' I asked Father Michael.

'We must return to Mexico City immediately and talk to the Tlatoani. He will know what to do next.'

On our way to the capital, we passed in front of a bank and then something came back to my mind: I had a key that could open a bank account supposedly set up by Anzules. I shared the information with my American priest and told him what I had found inside the safe deposit box.

'If I go back to the bank and ask them to show me who has set up *my* account, I should end up having a bank statement with some of Anzules' people's name on it. We could then cross reference these names with Miguel's knowledge of the people working with Anzules. That and the letter inside the box would prove he tried to bribe me with threats. As for the gold, the serial numbers would prove he was somehow involved in one of the largest-ever gold bullion robberies in the world, the 1983's Brinks Mat Robbery. He would then have to explain himself before a judge!'

'That's not a bad idea,' Father Michael agreed, as we were leaving the region of Santa Isabel Cholula. 'Not bad at all!'

119. Excerpt from *"The Aztlān Codex"*.

CHAPTER 1.

"THE LAST JOURNEY".

Because our last journey from our ancestral land to our new heaven was so long and so perilous, we decided to settle on an island and ask the Gods to show us the way. Their answer was as slow as the current of a small river, and so we also decided to choose our new Tlatoanis, the last one who would lead us before the rebirth of a new Mexica Empire. And he was known as Moctezuma III.

120. Is this some kind of joke?

2.51 p.m.

When we arrived at the *Banorte Merced* bank, we passed the automatic doors and headed to the reception desk. I introduced myself to a man in his fifties who was standing there in a grey suit.

'Hi there! My name is Jean Fleury and I would like to access my safe deposit box, please.'

The man didn't move at first, then he turned his head as if he wasn't interested. So I slowly repeated my request.

Still no reaction. But when the American priest repeated everything in Spanish, the man became talkative at last.

'He asks you to forgive him because he doesn't speak a word of English,' Father Michael immediately translated to me.

I gave him the account number that I still had on a piece of paper. He took it with him and slowly went to a personal bankers' computer behind the reception desk. He typed the number on the keyboard, clicked a few times on the screen and came back with a very different attitude. He looked quite concerned and anxious. Then he returned to us and started whispering.

'Is this some kind of joke?' he asked in a rough manner and in surprisingly good English.

'Excuse me?' I answered, astonished by the tone of his voice and the sudden change of language. 'What are you talking about? And by the way, I thought you didn't speak a word of English!'

Keeping his voice very low and leaning quite close to me and Father Michael, he took us away from the reception. He led us to a corner of the bank, far from the customers who were now staring at us from the comfortable-looking sofas.

'Well, as you might have noticed, this is a very respectable bank with very respectable customers,' he began, still whispering.

The bank receptionist was clearly referring to the three old wealthy Mexican women in fancy dresses who were chatting on the sofas, and five businessmen who were waiting at the tills.

'So, when I see two foreigners coming in our bank one dressed in a pair of jeans and a t-shirt, and the other as a priest, I tend to think pretending I don't speak English at all will deter them from staying in the building for too long…'

His explanation was rather elusive but he carried on whispering to me. 'Now, will you please tell me who you really are and what you really want? Because I know you are not Jean Fleury.'

'What are you talking about? I came in here two days ago to open my safe deposit box… Ask your colleague, DeMario…'

'Well, you must have come to the wrong bank or the wrong branch, because there isn't any DeMario working in this building! So if you don't mind, I will now ask you to leave the premises, before you force me to call the security guards…'

'Wait, can you at least confirm whether you have an account in this bank in the name of Jean Fleury?'

'Yes, we do have an account for Jean Fleury…'

I was exulted. I had proved I was right.

'…but according to our computers, Señor Jean Fleury died in 1527!' the receptionist continued, with a smile on his face. 'I think that someone must have hacked our database to make a joke…'

'Could you at least check the safe deposit box?' I insisted. 'There's a letter inside and also…'

'… and if you don't want me to call the police and get you both arrested for wasting my time and, most importantly, for having illegally accessed our computing system, I would suggest you immediately leave this building very quietly, without any trouble!'

I couldn't understand anything that was happening. First the farm had gone, then the little boy and his parents had vanished, and finally, the bank account had become a joke. Father Michael tried to reason with me. We needed to leave the bank otherwise we would really get into trouble.

'Getting arrested by the police is the last thing we need right now, Mister Duprés! We must return to the Temple and speak to the Tlatoani, quick!'

We left the bank and made our way back to the Aztlāns' headquarters by car. En route, I kept trying to understand what had happened at the bank.

'Come on, I mean, I met that guy, DeMario. He definitely worked in that bank. He looked and behaved like the bank receptionist we just met. I also saw my picture on their computer and it mentioned *"VIP Customer"*. Then we entered the safe, he made me sign something... and... well... he... didn't make any... problem with my... signature! I get it now: DeMario was from Anzules' people!'

Father Michael, who was driving quite fast in the empty streets of Mexico City, confirmed what he had also understood.

'In the same way as Anzules' men took the trouble to make you access the safe as if you were the owner of the bank account, they also removed everything that you could use against them if you were to return there. They would rather humiliate you in front of that man than let you prove they are involved in this conspiracy!'

'Once again, they've cleaned up everything behind them!'

121. Breaking News.

BTVB News, UK.

UK experts at the National Institute for Medical Research say that according to their preliminary analysis of the Swine Flu, the virus is a fairly mild strain, nowhere near as dangerous as the H5N1 Avian Flu strain. They believe that a further mutation is certainly needed in order for the virus to kill hundreds of thousands people in the world as it has been estimated by some, even though it is not possible at this point to accurately predict how the virus will continue to evolve.

The Swine Flu is the same type of virus as the seasonal
flu that circulates throughout the world every year and
kills roughly 0.1% of those infected (or higher in an
epidemic year).

122. Excerpt from *"The Aztlān Codex"*.

CHAPTER 4.

"KNOWING THE TRUTH".

Knowing the Truth was somehow an ordeal for the Eastern Eagle because he couldn't share his knowledge with anyone else since words would not be enough for the poor souls to believe him and understand the words.

And the Truth was one. And the Truth was everything. And the Truth was the sign. But knowing the Truth was also very dangerous, for the Dark Soul didn't want anyone to know everything.

One day, he, who led the people of Aztlān to the rebirth of their Empire, was lost in the sunny land. He wasn't lost because of the signs the gods had sent to him, but because he knew the Truth.

And he battled again against the darkest creatures of the Dark Soul, but this time, they pushed him away from the rays of light, killed his white horse, then cut his wrists, grabbed his heart, and eventually defeated him. As he received the news, the Dark Soul exulted and thought he could finally conquer the rest of the world.

123. The best-of.

3.33 p.m.

Father Michael was driving too fast for my taste, but he assured me that we needed to get back to the Temple before Anzules' men caught us.

The effects of the paranoia created by the mass coverage of the media were obvious. In front of us, the streets were empty of people and cars. Father Michael told me that even though it was really hot and sunny outside, no one would risk themselves going out even to buy a carton of milk at the supermarket, not with the virus in the air. Except maybe at La Merced.

Father Michael was a nice chap, very kind, and very understanding. Speaking to him was a bit like speaking to my own father. He was always smiling, very polite, and wasn't rude like the Aztlāns' leader. I felt that I could trust him with my little secret.

'Throughout my investigation, I have been keeping a diary on my iPhone every day. Everything I have seen, everything I have heard, it's all in there! One part is a written diary, and the other part is made of recordings like an audio diary. Every day, I have been recording all my conversations, to edit them to short conversations of three or four minutes, in the evening.'

'That's clever!' answered the priest He was trying to grab his mobile phone that had just fallen by his seat somewhere along the door, leaving him only one hand on the wheel and one eye on the road.

'This diary is a valuable source of information and if anything was to happen to me, it would automatically be sent to somebody I trust by email...'

'Does that mean you are currently recording this conversation as well?' He smiled.

'Well, yes...' I smiled back.

I actually needed to reset the system as I had programmed the timer two days ago for the wrong date. The sending date was set for 3rd May 2010, instead of 2009! Also, since Alicia was now Anzules' prisoner,

I couldn't send the diary to her email any longer. I grabbed my iPhone and tried to connect to the application to change the date and the recipient. As for Father Michael, he finally managed to grasp his telephone and started dialling Moctezuma's number to let him know that we were back in the capital.

Suddenly, coming from nowhere two black cars appeared across the street, right in front of us at a crossroad. They were completely still. I quickly recognised the model of the two cars: Mazda. Anzules' men! Four men in black were standing in front of the first vehicle.

Our car was going so fast that Father Michael had no choice but to brake as much as he could and try to avoid the car by turning the wheel to the left. This caused our car to slide sideways onto the other lanes of the road at first, then spin round three, four, five times…

The priest lost control of the vehicle. When I turned to him, I saw his seat belt hanging loose and I realised that he had lost consciousness, after hitting his window. As we hit one of the Mazdas, he got abruptly thrown through the car.

I couldn't contain my fear. I was absolutely terrified, and in my panic, I undid my own seatbelt. Unfortunately, it wasn't the end. Pushed against a small car parked in the street, the car ended up in the crossroad in the path of a large speeding fire truck that was certainly going to attend a fire somewhere in the city, judging by its sirens blaring. I literally collided into it. The car instantly caught fire. Through the broken rear mirror, I could see the fire now raging at the back of the vehicle.

If the driver's airbag inflated, mine didn't. As my seatbelt was undone, my body was loose in the car and my head first smashed violently against the side window, then the front windscreen. I had blood on my hands, my jeans, literally everywhere.

The smells of burning and smoke were so strong in there that breathing was becoming more and more difficult. If I didn't die from the cuts or the burns, I was going to die of asphyxia! I needed to escape, but how could I? When I hit the other car, a large piece of metal perforated my door pinning both my legs.

As the car was still spinning, I glimpsed Father Michael's body unanimated on the macadam. The car finally stormed against two other parked cars, lacerating two unfortunate pedestrians, and finished its deadly journey by smashing into the shop window of a small café, probably killing any living thing inside.

At last the car stopped moving. The fire was quickly spreading. There were maybe a dozen bodies lying on the floor everywhere in front of the car. The ceiling had fallen down and electrical wires were hanging loose, sparking. I could only see blood everywhere inside and outside the car.

More and more flames suddenly appeared from under the bonnet of the car. I started to see my life passing in front of my eyes in a flash. It was very much like *"a best of Jean-Baptiste Duprés"*. I was revisiting some of the most memorable moments of my life with images and sounds, and some flashing intervals…

I first saw the accident, then my meeting with Anzules in the jazz club, the first visit at the farm, meeting Alicia at the Basilica… Then the flashing intervals accelerated… My first day in Mexico City, my two previous investigations in Iraq and in Cuba with Carlos, my very first date with Sarah at *Le Bernardin*, my move to London to work as a foreign correspondent for AFP… The intervals were getting shorter and shorter… My thirtieth birthday party with all my friends from Carcassonne, my joy watching Olympique de Marseille win the Champions league in Munich, my first car: a Fiat Punto that collapsed after two days, and my first time: with Virginie Monteil behind the trees in Rue des Remparts. Then came my school days: playing truant in secondary school to be a DJ on the local radio, my happy family before my parents' divorce, my first day at the nursery school: crying all day long and asking for my mum, my mother looking at me for the very first time when I was born…

Then a long flash. Many voices talking at the same time. Sirens. Radio. Then silence. Blackout. Everything was dark. My eyes were closed. I opened my eyes. Another flash. The last one.

The car exploded.

124. Breaking News.

1st May 2009.

MexCity News 24, MEXICO.
The most violent car accident in the capital in years could well be a criminal investigation!

As many as nine people witnessed a totally violent car accident yesterday afternoon in central Mexico City that is thought to be of a criminal nature.

A Mexico City Police Department spokeswoman said: "Police were called at 03.47 p.m. yesterday afternoon after reports of a car accident involving a firefighters' truck and four cars, in Calle José María Pino Suárez, in the borough of Cuauhtémoc. Police officers, firefighters and Critical Air (helicopter emergency medical service) attended the scene. Five young men and one elderly woman suffering from burns and minor injuries were taken by the Ambulance Service to the closest hospital. A fifty-year-old priest, whose condition is still critical, was taken to hospital by helicopter. Fourteen other people were pronounced dead at the scene, including a thirty-six-year-old French male suffering from major burns and massive cuts, who was pronounced dead by the Ambulance Service. For each victim, next-of-kin have been informed. Road closures will remain in place until further notice, as we suspect that the accident did not occur randomly. A murder enquiry has now been launched to understand why this accident happened. A post mortem will take place in due course."

A spokesman for the City Mayor said he was assisting the police with the investigation into the accident. He also added, "Four men seen on CCTV outside two black Mazdas in the middle of the street where the accident happened were being sought by the detectives."

Any witnesses or anyone with information relevant to the investigation should immediately call the police on 061.

*"There will come a time when you believe
everything is finished.
Yet that will be the beginning."*
– Louis L'Amour (1908 – 1988)

CHAPTER 14. ALICIA'S DIARY

End [noun] – the last and final part of something that
is complete.

(Excerpt from the Storyteller Dictionary)

125. Another story.

Day 333 – 3rd May 2010, 11.22 a.m.

Until this morning, I thought that living as far as possible from
Rodrigo Stefano Borgia Anzules, the man I married in September 2007 in
Honolulu, was the best thing I had ever done in my life.

Sharing a tiny flat with a Korean girl who was also working at the
only fast-food one could find in central Kristiansand seemed to be a very
good idea. Especially because no one here knew, nor was interested in
knowing who I was and what my background was. Norway was a very low
profile type of country. And that certainly fitted me.

I wasn't completely disconnected from the wide *outside* world
though. I still browsed the Internet on a laptop, and I still accessed my
emails. But thanks to a friend, a professional hacker, I had managed to get
myself hidden, and most importantly, untraceable whenever I was
connected online. My escape from my husband's gang a year ago, and my

runaway since then hadn't been easy to cope with. Mainly because I knew that he and his men were still out there looking for me…

Until this morning, thus, I was at last living a well-deserved peaceful life again, in this country. But today, I received an email that made me rethink everything that had happened in Mexico.

We have all heard stories about the number of years it took for some letters, like love letters sent by soldiers to their fiancée or wife, to finally reach their destination. Well, I received an email almost a year later. It had been sent to me on 3rd May 2009 and it came from Jean-Baptiste Duprés' email account!

126. The email.

Inbox – doctorvanity1918@gmail.com

from	**unknown sender**
sender time	**Sent at 00:01 (GMT-07:00).**
	Current time there: 04:22.
to	**"Me" <doctorvanity1918@gmail.com>**
date	**03 May 2009 00:01**
subject	**Key to my Diary**

Dear Alicia,

If you ever read this email, it means that something very bad happened to me here in Mexico. So, I really hope that you never have to read it! ;)

In the event that you do receive this email, I first need to explain why you can still read my mail even though I am gone. When sending this email, I am using an online programme that allows me to send emails with the ability to have them sent at any date I choose in the future.

So, if you are reading this right now, it means that I was not able to change the date of sending, which I have been changing every week since the day I met you at the Basilica.

Why did I choose you as the recipient of this email? Simply because I trust you. Because I know that you will do the right thing with its content, so that everybody finally knows where the virus really came from, and maybe even more importantly, so that Anzules finally pays for his crime.

You will find underneath my explanations an Internet link, as well as a username and a password. The link is the address of my online diary. It is an audio and written diary. There, you will find all the recordings that I have made during my investigation on the virus (at least 50 hours, after editing) and I have also confined all my thoughts in writing.

My written diary could be used to convict Anzules, but it wouldn't be enough. That's why I hope you will find the strength to give evidence in a tribunal, because you have witnessed a lot of things and heard a lot too. As for my recordings, some of them would certainly get a lot of interest, especially if they are played in a tribunal.

The link to my diary is: www.jeanbaptistedupres.com
The username is: eMancipation@2514
The password is: univerSity0405-@

Alicia, you now have a real opportunity to get Anzules convicted, and put him in jail for a very long time for the horrible crime he has committed in creating the virus and spreading it all over the world. Please, don't let it go!

Finally, thank you for helping me with this difficult and dangerous investigation. I wish you all the best for the future.

Best regards,

Jean-Baptiste.

2 attachments — Download all attachments

smiley.gif 74K View Download
email-alicia.doc 156K View as HTML Open as a Google document
Download

127. The decision.

So, that was it. Jean-Baptiste Duprés had gone to meet his maker and left me with his secret diary that could incriminate my future ex-husband in the Swine Flu case.

I now had to make a serious decision. I could either ignore the email and stay away from the world, staying low-profile and hidden in Norway, or send the diary to the authorities and lose my quiet life and my serenity to give evidence in what could become the most documented trial of modern history.

Did I really want to get involved again? Did I really want to face Anzules again? Did I really want to jeopardise my new peaceful life in Kristiansand? I had to think more. Maybe I need some kind of sign?

128. Breaking News.

```
MexCity News 24, MEXICO.
Judge says Rodrigo S.B. Anzules isn't responsible for
French journalist's death!
```

It was a year ago, on April 30, 2009, that 18 people died in the most violent car accident Mexico City has seen for years.

Even though many witnesses could recall that two black Mazda cars belonging to billionaire Rodrigo S.B. Anzules were involved and clearly the cause of the accident, Honourable Judge Arellano Delgado said that Anzules could not be seen as responsible for the deaths of all 18 people. "It was not manslaughter. It was just bad luck," he simply stated to justify his decision to acquit him. "How could Señor Anzules be at all guilty of a terrible and unfortunate car accident? There are car accidents every day all over the country… does that make Señor Anzules responsible for all of them too?"

When asked by an American journalist whether the wealth and political acquaintances of Anzules had been taken into consideration when making his decision, the judge's demeanour became like a provoked lion. "Was Señor Anzules driving any of the cars involved? The answer is no!" he answered angrily. "Was Señor Anzules anywhere to be seen near or at the scene of the accident? The answer again is no! How could I put an innocent man in jail, a man well known for his generosity and loyalty towards the Mexicans and our society in general? Eighteen innocent people died in that very unfortunate accident a year ago. I would like to ask you all, journalists, to please give their family a rest once and for all!"

Most foreign observers and newspapers have described the trial of Rodrigo S.B. Anzules as a complete parody of justice, with endless errors of procedure, witnesses unwilling to give evidence because of death threats, CCTV recordings edited, documents and proofs vanishing, etc. The Impartial Newspaper, in the United Kingdom, said about the verdict: "It was just another display of what corruption means in a country like Mexico, where barons can do as they wish as long as they pay the price."

As for the French authorities, a spokeswoman of the French Foreign Minister present at the tribunal said that, for them, "It was obvious from day one of the seven-week long trial that the judge was not going far enough to address the case and to understand what had actually happened on 30 April 2009 to Jean-Baptiste Duprés and the other victims." She added that the French government would now urge its Mexican counterpart to explain why Judge Delgado authorised Rodrigo S.B. Anzules to stay out of jail, not to serve any kind of home confinement, and allowed him to travel abroad and to keep running his business, Anzules Group, for the whole duration of the trial. "All the judge's decisions," concluded the spokeswoman for the French Foreign Minister, "are deemed by the French government as utterly unacceptable."

129. Breaking News.

Shares Watcher, USA.

Anzules Group's stock price at the New York Stock Exchange rapidly went down to $15 per share on the first day of billionaire Rodrigo S.B. Anzules' seven-week trial. The fall came despite analysts saying they doubted Anzules would be convicted and sent to jail given Anzules' infamous reputation in the corruption world.

Now that the trial has ended, everyone recognises that the experts were right for two reasons. First, Anzules escaped a jail sentence and came out of the trial as a great winner and a respectable man – in the eye of the judicial system, at least. Second, shares in Anzules Group this morning rose to their highest level in nearly five years, after investors reacted to the judge's verdict to clear Anzules of all charges.

Let's be honest: the trial wasn't actually a bad thing for Anzules' billfold! He has ended up even richer than before the trial!

Note from the editor: Anzules Group's chairman, president and CEO is founder Rodrigo S.B. Anzules himself. In 1996, Rodrigo Anzules founded Grupo Anzules in Guatemala. In 2000, the company moved to the USA and changed its name to Anzules Group. On September 15, 2000, Anzules Group went public on the New York Stock Exchange under the ticker symbol AZG. The initial public offering was set at $10 per share, and rallied to $90 by the end of trading, making Rodrigo S.B. Anzules an instant billionaire. Anzules was then and continues to be the majority shareholder, with a commanding 92% control of voting power in the company.

130. Seating in Los Pinos.

When I read the news about Anzules and the way he had once again escaped justice, I felt like I just couldn't stay here saying nothing about what had happened in Mexico last year. The judge's decision was portraying him as a respectable gentleman, which he wasn't. And everybody knew it. But once again, nobody would stop him. Nobody ever dared do anything to stop him reaching the skies, making more and more money, and grabbing more and more power.

I knew that his dream was to become president of Mexico. He told me once that not being a natural-born citizen of Mexico himself wouldn't be a real problem as his political friends would vote in a bill to change that requirement to hold office before the election took place. If he became president of Mexico by cheating the votes, nobody would say a word. Anzules would thus peacefully have a seat in *Los Pinos*.

I felt so angry and so useless. But there wasn't anything that I could do! Well… Maybe…

131. Breaking News.

26th May 2010, 03.34 p.m.

**The Impartial Newspaper, UK.
Guatemalan billionaire Anzules goes on trial again.**

What is going on in Mexico? Less than a month ago, a judge declared Guatemalan billionaire Rodrigo S.B. Anzules not guilty of manslaughter for the death of eighteen people in a street of the capital, Mexico City.

Today, the founder of Latin America's second largest company, and a few weeks ago Latin America's richest man, is going on trial again amid the tightest security ever seen in a Mexican court. Anzules, 35, chairman, president, and CEO of Anzules Group, now faces charges of commercial and administrative briberies, major business offences, extortion, and judicial and executive power corruption. But the main charges that Anzules faces are without a doubt murder and crimes against humanity. Crimes against humanity for the creation and deliberate spread of the pandemic H1N1 Swine Flu virus in Mexico and the rest of the globe, which killed over 18,000 people across the world. Rodrigo Anzules has been in detention in Mexico City since 08/05.

Mexican officers had tracked Anzules to the Big Apple with a warrant issued by the Mexican authorities to arrest him, but they were unable to make the arrest themselves out of their jurisdiction. The Interpol National Central Bureau in Washington D.C. acted as a liaison between the Mexican and the United States law-enforcement agencies. Anzules was then arrested on board a plane to Hong Kong before take-off by FBI officers at JFK airport on 06/05 and kept in custody for two days.

Because of the very serious allegations of crimes against humanity, the International Criminal Court got involved, but the United States, being critical of the court and having unsigned its statute, claimed that they had no legal obligations to extradite Anzules to The Hague in the Netherlands for him to be judged there. Since Mexico is a state party of the ICC, the Mexican authorities accepted holding the trial in Mexico City. The US Attorney General immediately accepted the Mexican extradition mandate and handed over the billionaire to Mexico.

It took prosecutors two weeks to finally bring charges against him, and they said they have now collected so much evidence against him that six police vans were needed to bring all the paperwork to the court, in the Mexican capital.

Alicia Thomson-Anzules, the Guatemalan's estranged wife is scheduled to give evidence against her husband tomorrow morning. According to the prosecutors, she has supplied them with "hundreds of confidential documents about Anzules' corruption system and his direct link to the H1N1 virus." She copied the documents in secret, at Anzules Group's headquarters, in New York, between September 2008 and March 2009. "Thanks to these documents, her crucial testimony, and a surprise final element, Anzules won't escape jail this time!" declared a very confident prosecutor.

Rodrigo Anzules' trial will be the first in a series after hundreds of senior officials, including ministers, members of parliament, mayors, lawyers, prosecutors, judges, and even senior officers in the police and the military have been questioned by the five most ruthless anti-corruption judges in the country about their connection to the billionaire's corruption network.

Anzules, who used to show off his white Porsche Cayman S everywhere, arrived at the court this morning in a dark and dirty prison van, escorted by eight police cars, five police vans, and four helicopters. Why so much security? Maybe to make sure that none of his friends attempt to make him vanish before he can attend his trial.

In Mexico, the trial that is expected to last twelve weeks is already being seen by the Mexicans as their pre-summer soap opera, in which Anzules is the star. As they entered the court this morning, Anzules' lawyers said that the billionaire, who faces up to 30 years in jail, "…contests the evidence and will fight every minute of the trial to keep his name clear of all these false and horribly absurd accusations against him."

132. My testimony.

27th May 2010, 01.11p.m.

So, I did it. I told them the whole story this morning. I was so nervous at first, but then I told them everything I knew about the bribery system used by Anzules Group to win markets everywhere in Mexico and elsewhere on the American continent, about the corrupted judges, journalists, police officers, etc.

I told them everything, along with supporting evidence that I had collected in the company's headquarters in New York, after discovering what Anzules was planning to do with the Swine Flu virus. I had scanned all the documents and stored them online in my Office Live Workspace account, where nobody else could access them.

Then to finish, the cherry on the cake, I told them about the Swine Flu virus. I explained what Anzules wanted to use it for, but also his fight against the Vatican hidden organisation, and his fight against the Aztlān Project organisation. I once again had enough evidence, in particular documents signed by Anzules himself, to support my testimony. Then we read some passages of Jean-Baptiste Duprés' personal diary and played some of his recordings too. Especially the one at the jazz club when Jean-Baptiste met Anzules.

I felt so much better afterwards. I felt like I had done the world a huge favour by talking on behalf of all those who couldn't because they were too afraid of him and his people.

My lawyer and the prosecutors told me that within the next three weeks, I would be called again to be cross-examined, by Anzules' lawyers this time. They would try to challenge me by all means, discredit me, and certainly try to ruin my reputation. In a nutshell, make my life hell. I couldn't wait!

Then other witnesses would also give evidence after me, and maybe bring other documents for the jury's consideration too. And finally about three weeks later, the jury would take a decision, and hopefully…

As I was talking to my lawyer in the corridors of the court after giving evidence, I came across a priest who introduced himself to me as Moctezuma. He was the leader of the *Aztlān Project* organisation, who Jean-Baptiste Duprés mentioned in his diary. He simply came to thank me for my courage and my tenacity in getting Anzules finally trialled. He also said that Jean-Baptiste had not died in vain. Then after two minutes of conversation, he left.

I couldn't agree more. Jean-Baptiste had shown me the way. He was brave and fearless. He went through so many things in less than a week of investigation that I could only admire the man.

I was very proud to be able to say that I had met the great Jean-Baptiste Duprés.

133. Breaking News.

Shares Watcher, USA.

Anzules Group's latest attempts to limit the financial damage from the cataclysmic trial of chairman Rodrigo S.B. Anzules in Mexico, who faces up to thirty years in jail if found guilty of crimes against humanity, suffered a massive blow this morning when Alicia Thomson-Anzules, Anzules' estranged wife, gave evidence against him.

Anzules Group, which had no insurance in place for the unexpected trial, is now trying to claim up to $950m through a policy held by its founder, chairman, and CEO, Rodrigo Anzules himself, who Anzules Group's shareholders blame for the company's catastrophic stock price fall at the New York Stock Exchange, Shares Watcher can reveal.

In a TV appearance on the KNL Lunchtime News today, Ken Williams, Anzules Group's vice-president, has hit back at critics of the company's alleged bribery practice, saying "They all ought to remember that the group is very big and very important for the economy of Mexico and the Americas." He added, "More than 25,000 employees depend every day on the well-being of the company all around the world, which is really not negligible!"

As Guatemalan billionaire Anzules prepares to be questioned today for the first time by the three prosecutors about his links to the H1N1 virus, Ken Williams also said, "Everything that can be done will be done," to save the company from a disaster, "even if that means our chairman has to stand down from his position."

Over the phone from Mexico, one of Anzules' lawyers immediately denied that he ever thought about or ever will be stepping down.

Anzules Group's shares price had already started to tumble yesterday, dragged along by the world markets with the FTSE 100 index in London falling by 2.54%, the Dax 30 in Frankfurt by 2.7%, and the CAC 40 in Paris by 3.5%. But the markets were more worried about the rising tensions between the two Koreas, as well as the EU's financial crisis that could well postpone a global economic recovery than the outcome of the most talked-about trial in recent times.

134. Breaking News.

13th August 2010, 06.28 p.m.

The Impartial Newspaper, UK.
Guatemalan billionaire found guilty of crimes against humanity.

When Honourable Judge Rodolfo González Camarena asked the jury to retire and come back with a clear and unanimous verdict, he certainly didn't think it would take them less than two hours to take a decision. But that's what happened just a few minutes ago. And when everybody came back inside the courtroom to hear the jury's verdict, not even a mosquito would have dared fly as everything was hanging upon the Judge's lips.

He first read to himself the jury's verdict written on a large piece of paper and then read it out loud: "It is the decision of the jury of this Court for the Federal District of Mexico to award a verdict to the claimants and declare the defendant guilty on three charges. The sentence of Rodrigo Stefano Borgia Anzules will go as follows. First, and foremost, Rodrigo

Stefano Borgia Anzules will be sentenced to thirty years in jail for crimes against humanity, for deliberately, consciously, maliciously, and with evil intent, creating and spreading the deadly virus H1N1 through one of his companies. A virus that, as of today, killed over 18,000 people in the world. The defendant then lobbied very strongly for the sale of his company's antiviral drugs and later for the sale of its H1N1 vaccines, with the help of insiders at the World Health Organization, making a very large profit at a time when every other company in the world was in the middle of a recession. Second, Rodrigo Stefano Borgia Anzules will be sentenced to fifteen years in jail for ordering the death of a man, the French journalist Jean-Baptiste Duprés. If it is not clear whether the defendant had ordered the death of Jean-Baptiste Duprés on the day he actually died in a car accident, it is very clear through witnesses giving evidence that the defendant was constantly saying he wanted the French journalist dead, and he also said so through a recording at a jazz club in New York. Lastly, Rodrigo Stefano Borgia Anzules will be sentenced to fifteen years in jail for corrupting the course of justice, for intimidation caused by life threats, for bribery and corruption at all levels of the administrative, military, and judicial systems in Mexico. This is the decision of this court. The trial is now over."

When the announcement was finished, the public in the room stood up. Most of them were clapping and shouting, and calling Anzules all the names under the sun. Four police officers immediately came to the fallen billionaire to put him in handcuffs and then ordered him to move towards a small door on the side of the courtroom. Alicia Thomson-Anzules and her lawyer walked out of the courthouse.

The prosecutors were delighted with the verdict, while Anzules' lawyers already announced they would "keep fighting for Rodrigo Anzules and appeal to the Supreme Court of Justice of the Nation", which is the highest federal court in Mexico.

135. The offer.

06.35 p.m.

I quickly left the court by a side door protected by the police, to avoid the media frenzy outside the building. After two minutes walking down the street, I noticed that a black Rolls Royce was slowly following my every step. When I eventually stopped, it stopped by my side. The passenger's tinted window slowly slid down and a man's face finally appeared at the window. It was an old priest with a small greyish beard and round John Lennon style glasses.

'May I have a word with you, Mrs Thomson-Anzules?' the man asked in English with a strong Italian accent, smiling.

'What do you want to talk about?' I replied, more worried about the dark clouds suddenly covering the sky. 'And who are you in the first place?'

'I would like to make you an offer that I am sure you won't refuse!' he replied, giving me a red patterned playing card.

'Look. I don't think you understand. I haven't got time for games, I'm sorry!' I declined the offer, without even wanting to know what it was all about.

The priest then turned the card over to reveal a mysterious, but somewhat familiar symbol: the sacred *Tonalpohualli* Mexica Calendar.

'What if I tell you that I could take you right now to the Vatican and show you a secret place, highly protected, where the unique and enigmatic Codex Teōtīhuacān is currently resting, and that I would like you to take all the time needed to read it peacefully and decrypt its unbreakable meaning for me?'

I looked him in the eyes. Was the old bearded man bluffing? His accent seemed genuine and his words too. I doubted that he was one of the cardinals of *In Pectore*. These guys never did their own dirty jobs!

What about the offer? I was interested in the Codex Teōtīhuacān when I was working for the institute here in Mexico City, and I always dreamt about being able to see it, examine it. Because of the mysteries surrounding its meaning, I had always considered it the most important Codex of all.

The old me was certainly interested, but what about the new me? Did I really want to get involved in some other complicated story? What new adventures would my involvement get me into this time?

An Italian priest in Mexico offering me to decrypt the Codex for him… I knew that it wasn't going to be that simple. The priest was obviously not going to tell me the whole story anyway.

But I had had enough of secrets for now. I had just risked my life, put other people's lives in danger, and forever lost someone who I trusted with my life, all for a virus. I wasn't prepared to do the same for a Codex!

So I gave his card back to the priest and just declined the offer very politely, walking away from the car. The priest didn't insist any longer and didn't try to follow me either. I disappeared in the small streets of the neighbourhood of Tlatilco, which means *"the place of hidden things"* in Nahuatl language.

In this beautiful city of Mexico, the streets were full of children playing. In the middle of the street, Rafael and his friends were playing soccer with tin cans, running around and shouting, as they imagined he had scored the victory goal for Mexico at the next World Cup. On the pavement, Angelica and her friends were looking at the noisy boys while playing quietly with their dolls, pretending that Barbie was going to have Ken's seventh baby.

As they were innocently having fun under the sun, with some Mexican music playing on a radio, they were oblivious to the fact that a very dangerous man had just been put in jail for a very long time, and he would never again be a threat to their lives or that of their families…

245

THE END

*"No amount of guilt can change the past,
and no amount of worrying can change the future."*
– Unknown source

ABOUT THE AUTHOR

British-born historian and anthropologist. Research Fellow at the Institute of Ethnology, Mexican Academy of Sciences, and Member of the National Institute of Indigenous Peoples, Mexico City. She has been living in Mexico for over 15 years.

Her Twitter account is: @JosephaWQuint

CONTENTS